To

Frances Harrick

from

Mother + Daddy

Dec, 6th 1944.

THE ALICE AND JERRY BOOKS

READING FOUNDATION SERIES

THE
FIVE-AND-A-HALF
CLUB

MARGERY BIANCO

Author of
"A Street of Little Shops,"
"The Good Friends," and
"More About Animals"

and

MABEL O'DONNELL

Elementary Supervisor, Aurora, Illinois

Illustrated by Margaret Ayer

ROW, PETERSON AND COMPANY

NEW YORK CITY   EVANSTON, ILLINOIS   SAN FRANCISCO

Contents

Copyright, 1942. Row, Peterson and Company. 2064
Registered in U.S. Patent Office.   Printed in the U.S.A.
International and Imperial Copyright secured
All rights reserved for all countries, including the right of translation.

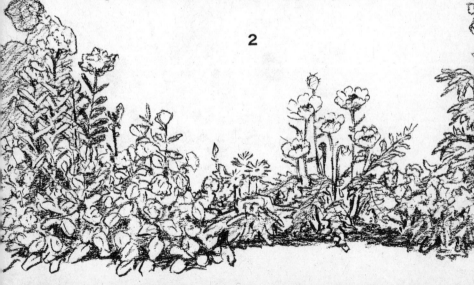

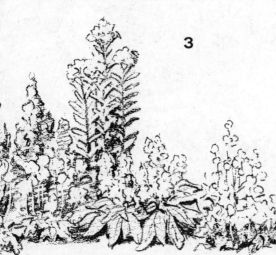

How It All Started

School was over.

For weeks the children had been looking forward to the summer vacation. They could hardly wait for those long summer days with no more hurrying off after breakfast and no more homework in the evening. There would be nothing to do but to play and enjoy themselves from morning to night.

At least, that was how it seemed to
Bill and Martha Strong and the Baker
twins and Sally Green, the little group
of friends who lived at the far end of
town. Going to and from school together
the last few days, they had talked of
nothing but vacation and what good times
they were going to have. It would be
just too wonderful.

And for two weeks it was wonderful.
Then the same thing happened that
happens nearly every year after school
is out. There came a day when all the
excitement was over, and there was
nothing at all left to do.

Every boy and girl knows what these days are like, and every mother knows, too. Mrs. Strong and Mrs. Baker were sure that there must be plenty of things to do if the children would only go and do them. Both mothers were tired of seeing Bill and Ann and Martha and Jimmy always hanging round the house. They were tired of hearing them say, every few minutes, "I wish I had something to do!"

"Here you've been talking about vacation for weeks and weeks," Mrs. Strong said to Bill and Martha, "and now that it is here, all you do is sit around the house. Why don't you get some interesting book if you can't find anything else to do?"

"I've read all my books," Bill said.

"Then you can go out and rake the yard."

"That isn't any fun," said Bill.

Over at the Baker house it was just the same. Neither Ann nor Jimmy could settle down to anything.

"Why don't you play outdoors?" their mother asked them. "You should be outdoors all day long this lovely weather."

But Ann and Jimmy didn't want to be outdoors. They didn't want to be indoors, either. They did not know what they wanted. They wandered in and out, a dozen times in an hour, until they nearly drove their mother wild.

By the end of the second day both mothers knew that this kind of thing couldn't go on. But it was Mrs. Strong who put an end to it. As soon as Bill and Martha came down to breakfast with that "what-can-we-do-now" look on their faces, they met a surprise.

"Now today is my busy day," their mother said, "and I can't have you two around all the time. I want you to go out and to stay out. If you can't find something to amuse yourselves, don't come to me!"

Ten minutes later a sad-looking pair walked slowly down the back steps. They felt very sorry for themselves. If Mother had so many things to do, why couldn't they help her? Or why couldn't they watch her? Watching Mother was always fun. But Mother had said to stay out, and she meant it. Bill and Martha stood and looked at each other. Neither said a word, but they must have been thinking the same thoughts, for suddenly both turned in the direction of Sally Green's house. Sally could always think of something.

Before long they were in the Greens' kitchen. Mrs. Green was getting potatoes ready for dinner, and Sally was drying the breakfast dishes. There was nothing for Bill and Martha to do but stand, first on one foot and then on the other, and watch.

Bill and Martha liked Mrs. Green. All the children did. She was Sally's grandmother. But she didn't look much like a grandmother. She had dark hair and twinkly brown eyes and a quick way of talking and moving that didn't make her seem old at all.

"I wish we lived by the seashore, or out in the country, or some place where a fellow could have some fun," began Bill. "Round here there's never anything to do that's any good. I get tired doing the same things over and over. I just wish we could go off and live some place all by ourselves."

"Well, why don't you?" asked Mrs. Green, looking up from the kitchen table.

Mrs. Green had a way of saying unexpected things like that. It was one reason why the boys and girls all liked her. Today she sounded as if she knew just how it felt to be nine years old and restless, and not to know what to do with one's self.

"Live by ourselves? Why, we couldn't!" cried Bill in a surprised voice.

Mrs. Green took another potato from the pan and began to take off the skin.

"Of course," she said, "I don't mean live by yourselves all the time. But you could find something to do all by yourselves. Just start something of your own, something that would keep you busy."

Now this was just what Billy's and Martha's mother had said all day yesterday and the day before that. It was just what Mrs. Baker was still saying at her house. But somehow, when Mrs. Green said it, it sounded different. It sounded pleasant and almost exciting.

"Do you mean a club?" Martha asked.

"Something of that kind," answered Mrs. Green.

"A club!" cried Sally at once. "That would be grand! We could have meetings and everything. A club of our own would be just what we want."

Martha began to count.

"There will be Bill and Sally and Jimmy and Ann and me. That makes five."

"And Bobby Wells," Sally added.

"We can't have Bobby," said Bill. "He's too little."

"He isn't so little," said Mrs. Green. "He's nearly six."

"But he can't do all the things we do," said Bill.

"Why not?" asked Mrs. Green. "You don't know yet what you are going to do. So how do you know whether Bobby can do the same things or not? From what I have seen of Bobby, he is a very bright little boy. I don't think he will be any trouble at all, and I'm sure he will want to join. He won't have much fun playing alone if everyone else is in a club, will he?"

"Well, anyway—" Bill began.

"Anyway, we might have him part of the time," said Sally. "And I'll promise to look after him so that he won't be in the way."

So that was settled.

The next thing was to name the club. They thought of all kinds of names, but there was something wrong with each one. Sally thought that the Busy Bee Club would be a good name, but Bill didn't like it.

"We aren't going to be busy every minute," he said. "We want to have a good time. Anyway, it sounds like a girls' club. Why couldn't we call it the Lazybones Club?"

"We could, but we won't," answered Sally. "I don't feel lazy, and you wouldn't if you had something to do."

It was Martha who finally named the club. "Why not call it the Five-and-a-Half Club?" she said. "There are five of us, and the half can be Bobby because he's the smallest."

The others all laughed, and poor Martha's cheeks turned very red. She was younger than Billy and Sally, and she didn't like to have them think that the things she said were foolish. Bill did think so. "That's a foolish kind of name," he said.

"I don't think it is," said Mrs. Green, and she smiled at Martha. Martha began to feel happier.

"I think it is a fine name," said Sally, who did not see why Bill should want everything his own way. "Only we must never let Bobby know that the half means him."

And so the Five-and-a-Half Club it was.

A Bargain

The next important thing was a meeting place. Bobby and Martha thought that they could meet at each other's houses, but the older children were against the idea. They wanted a place of their own, and they wouldn't be happy until they had one.

Bill longed for a hut, and when he couldn't have a hut, he wanted a tent. Mrs. Green found two old blankets and a clothesline and helped them fix up a tent in her back garden. But the tent was not big enough for everyone to sit in at the same time. Someone always had to sit outside. Also, the blankets were likely to fall down on their heads at any minute. And, of course, there were rainy days when that kind of tent was no good. They had to run into the house or stand in puddles of water. Even Bill could see that the tent wasn't a good idea. A new meeting place had to be found.

Next door to Sally's house was a little white house where Mr. and Mrs. Riley lived. Back of this house was Mr. Riley's garden, and right at the end of the garden was a shed. It used to be the Rileys' woodshed before Mr. Riley built his new shed close to the kitchen door.

One day after a big rain the boys and girls were all gathered outside their tent, looking sadly at the wet blankets. It would take hours for the sun to dry them. Back of Mrs. Green's currant bushes the tin roof of Mr. Riley's shed flashed in the sunlight. It was dry and shining and clean.

"I wish Mr. Riley would let us use that old shed of his," said Jimmy longingly.

"Maybe he would if we asked him," answered Martha. But her voice didn't sound very hopeful.

Mr. Riley was a queer old gentleman. Sometimes he was friendly, and sometimes he wasn't. You could never be sure just how he was feeling, because of his leg. When it was bad weather, his leg hurt him; and when Mr. Riley's leg worried him, his temper was likely to worry him, also. It was almost as if he kept his temper right there in his leg. His temper had surely been worrying him last week when Bill's ball flew up on to Mr. Riley's kitchen roof. How cross Mr. Riley had been!

"I think Sally should ask," Billy said. "She's the biggest, and she lives right next door."

"If we had that shed," said Jimmy, "maybe we could get some paint and fix it all up inside. I should think if someone told Mr. Riley we were going to paint it and make it look nice, he'd be glad to let us use it."

19

"And we needn't even go through his garden," Ann added. "There's a broken place in the fence, and we can get through that way. Mr. Riley wouldn't even see us."

The more they talked about the shed, the more they felt that if they could not use Mr. Riley's shed, it wouldn't be much fun having a club at all. They wondered what Mr. Riley would say if they asked him, and just what would be the best way to begin.

Not one of the boys and girls wanted to go and ask Mr. Riley. They were afraid that he would say no; and once he said no, it would be all over. Even Sally was a little bit afraid of old Mr. Riley. But at last she said that she would go and ask him.

She talked to her grandmother that evening while they were washing the supper dishes. Mrs. Green didn't believe in putting things off. She said, "If I were you, I'd go right over and ask him now. He can't bite your head off!"

Sally went across to the next-door garden. Mr. Riley had just come home from his work at the railroad yard and was out in his garden. He went there the first thing when he got home from work every evening. He had a fine garden, and he took good care of it.

Sally did not know just how to begin. At last she said, "Your beans are coming along nicely, Mr. Riley."

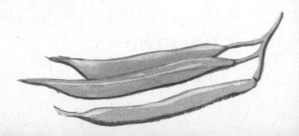

Now, if Sally had thought for a whole week, she could not have thought of anything that would please old Mr. Riley more. He leaned on his rake and smiled.

"They are," he said. "They're coming along fine. If only the cutworms don't get them!"

Sally had once lived in the country, so she knew all about cutworms. She knew that they live underground, and she knew how much harm they can do in a garden. So it was easy to talk to Mr. Riley about cutworms. And from that, little by little, she worked round to talking about Mr. Riley's shed and what he was going to do with it.

"That shed, now," said Mr. Riley, stopping his work to look at it. "I thought I would pull it down. Looks kind of unsightly, that shed does, and it takes up room, too."

"It doesn't take up very much room," Sally said. "It would look all right if it was painted."

"Paint costs money," said Mr. Riley. "It's all I can do to keep my house painted, without painting that old shed."

Then Sally told him about the club.

"What?" cried Mr. Riley. "A pack of noisy young ones in my shed? No, thank you!"

"But we wouldn't be noisy," Sally promised. "We'd be very quiet."

"There's not a boy or girl in the world that can keep quiet," answered Mr. Riley. "And what's more, you'd be running all through my garden, too."

"No, we wouldn't, Mr. Riley," said Sally. "We'd go in and out through that hole in the fence. We wouldn't have to go through your garden at all."

Mr. Riley growled. He had forgotten that hole in the fence.

"And we could paint the shed up for you and make it all nice," Sally went on. "It would look much better than it does now. We'll do it if we can earn enough money to buy the paint. Then the paint, you see, would be your rent for letting us use the shed."

"Rent? Who's talking about rent?" And Mr. Riley began raking again, very busily. "I don't want to rent that shed. What I want to do is to pull it down."

"But if we did paint it for you, and made it look nice, maybe you wouldn't want to pull it down. It's still a good shed."

Mr. Riley growled again. It looked as though Sally was going to be a match for him. He went on raking harder than ever. Suddenly he stopped.

"I tell you what," he said. "I'm away all day, so it won't worry me. And Mrs. Riley spends most of her time in the house, so it won't worry her, if you'll be quiet. There'd be you and that Bill Strong and the Baker boy. We won't count the little girls and Bobby. But those two boys and you are plenty big enough to do a little work.

"Now, this garden is going to need weeding, and plenty of it, from now on. I'm not so good at weeding as I used to be. It gets me all tired out. If those boys want to keep my garden weeded — and I mean weeded — from now on, I guess I'll let you use the shed for your playhouse. If you want to spend your own money on painting it up, you can. But mind you — I don't want any mischief, and I won't have any noise! Now you run along and tell the boys what I've said."

"I will. And thank you very, very much, Mr. Riley."

If Sally thought that she had made a good bargain, so did Mr. Riley. He looked round at his garden. It looked nice now, but pretty soon the weeds would be coming up thick and fast. Those boys would have plenty to do if they were going to keep that garden the way he liked to see it!

Dollars and Cents

Right after breakfast next morning, the children ran over to look at their shed. What if it had blown down during the night? Or what if Mr. Riley had changed his mind? But there stood the shed safe and sound, and Mr. Riley was nowhere around. He had taken out his gardening tools, and the shed was all empty and ready.

There was plenty of room inside. Whoever had built that shed had made it big enough to hold wood for a whole winter. There was no wood in it now, except two or three logs in one corner. There was no window because woodsheds don't have windows; but when the door was opened wide, it let in all the air and sunshine that anyone could want. The children were delighted.

To be sure, there was a hole in the roof at one corner, but it was a small hole. It wouldn't matter. There were plenty of spider nests, too, for the spiders had been having it their own way all spring, with no one to trouble them.

Sally ran for a broom, Bill for a rake, and Jimmy for a basket. The boys and girls worked hard all morning. By noon they were hot and tired. But the shed was all cleaned out, the earth floor raked smooth, and the bits of old wood all picked up and carried away. Everyone was pleased but the spiders. They had gone hurrying away, much upset at losing their fine homes. Now they would have to begin life all over again somewhere else.

Martha stayed outside until the cleaning was over. She was afraid of spiders. She knew that they couldn't hurt her, but she was afraid of them all the same. She did not like the way their legs twinkled when they ran.

"Spiders are lucky," said Sally.

"If spiders are lucky," said Jimmy, "this is going to be a very lucky place!"

"The next thing to do," said Bill, "is to get this shed painted, inside and out."

Sally thought that if they could not buy paint, they might use whitewash. Whitewash did not cost so much, but it came off on one's clothes. Paint would be much better.

"How about wallpaper?" Ann asked.

"You can't put wallpaper outside," said Bill. "It would all wash off when it rains."

"We could put it inside," Ann said. Ann was all for wallpaper, the kind with roses on it.

"The first thing to do," said Jimmy, "is to put all our money together and see just how much we've got before we buy anything."

It was not much. Sally had seventeen cents, and Jimmy had twenty-four. Martha had nine pennies. Ann didn't have any money because she had been spending it all summer on candy. Bill had two dollars in his bank, but he was saving it to buy a bicycle. Besides, his bank was the kind that would open only when it had a whole five dollars inside.

"Banks don't count," said Sally. "Let's say that no one can take money out of a bank. If this club wants money, we will have to earn it. That way will be more fun."

"We could pick berries later on," Jimmy said.

"I get five cents a week for washing dishes," said Ann. "I can put that in."

"Mrs. Brooks gave me ten cents once for cutting the grass at her house," said Jimmy. "Maybe she would like me to do it every week. I guess there are a good many people who would like things done for them if we went round and asked."

While Ann and Jimmy were talking, Sally was busy with a pencil and paper. "Look," she said. "This shows just how much money we've got now." The children looked, and there on paper they read the following:

THE FIVE-AND-A-HALF CLUB

Sally	$ .17
Jimmy	.24
Martha	.09
Bill	.00
Ann	.00
Bobby	.00
	$ .50

It didn't look very well for Bill and Ann. Ann wished now that she had not bought all that candy. Bill felt a little mean about those two dollars in his bank. But all he said was, "I guess I can earn money. I can earn twenty-five cents a week, easy."

Sally counted up.

"There are five of us," said she. "Of course, we can't expect any help from Bobby. He's too little. But if each of the rest of us makes ten cents a week, we'll have a dollar in two weeks' time. A dollar should be enough to buy paint."

"I tell you what we'll do!" shouted Jimmy. "We'll go down to Mr. Wells's store and ask him. He sells paint. He sells wallpaper, too. He'll know how much they cost. Come on, let's go and ask him now!"

More Bargains

Mr. Wells was Bobby's father. His store was next to the post office. The boys liked it better than any other store in town, except the new Five-and-Ten. It had all kinds of interesting things in it, the kinds of things boys wanted. One could spend a whole afternoon in Mr. Wells's store, just looking round.

When the Five-and-a-Half Club went in today, Mr. Wells was busy waiting on a woman who wanted a new teakettle. Mr. Wells had plenty of teakettles. He had plenty of pots and pans and saucepans, too, and everything else one might need in a kitchen. He had taken down all his teakettles from the shelves, and the woman was looking at each one in turn and asking what it cost.

Mr. Wells was going to be busy for a long time. Anyone could see that. So the children walked past him, past all the new oilstoves and brooms and garden tools and boxes of nails, right to the far end of the store where Mr. Wells kept his paints and wallpaper.

People always took a long while making up their minds what to buy in Mr. Wells's store. It wasn't like the other stores. There nearly everyone was in a hurry. Here no one hurried, not even Mr. Wells himself.

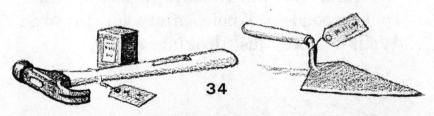

The back of the store was cool and dark. It smelled of paint and oil and new rope. The boys and girls didn't mind waiting. They looked at the rows and rows of paint cans up on the shelves. They read the tickets on the flashlights and hammers and other tools in the glass case under the counter. And they ran their hands, at least Ann did, over the rolls and rolls of wallpaper.

"If I get a dollar for my birthday," said Bill, "I'm going to buy one of those flashlights. That great big one there."

"I've got a flashlight," said Jimmy. "I'd like a jackknife. There's a beauty for seventy-five cents. But my birthday doesn't come until fall. That's nearly four months to wait."

At last Mr. Wells had finished with the teakettle woman. The boys asked him about paint.

"I've got all kinds of paint," said Mr. Wells. "What kind of paint do you want? Do you want inside paint, or do you want outside paint?"

"Which kind costs less?" Jimmy asked him.

"It isn't a question of cost," said Mr. Wells. "It's a question of where you want to use it."

Then he explained that outside paint is used for the outside of houses, and inside paint for rooms. Outside paint is made to stand rain and bad weather.

The boys told him about their clubhouse, and what they wanted to do.

"What you need is outside paint," Mr. Wells told them. "I have a very good barn paint. It comes in gray or red, and it costs a dollar and a half for a large can. One large can will paint three hundred square feet of wall. How big is your shed?"

Bill wasn't sure. He thought that it was about as long as from the end nail box to Mr. Wells's paint counter — maybe a little longer. And it was about as high — well, about as high as most sheds. If he stretched his arms up, he guessed he could just about touch the edge of the roof.

Jimmy thought that it was even bigger than that, but he couldn't be sure, either. For once, the girls hadn't a word to say.

Mr. Wells had a pretty good idea how big that shed was because his house was right at the back of Mr. Riley's house, and he could see Mr. Riley's shed any time from his kitchen window. But he thought that if the boys were going to do the work of painting it, they had better learn to go about it in the right way. And the first thing was to measure for themselves and find out just how much paint they would need.

"Three hundred square feet sounds big to me," said Bill. "Maybe we'll need only a small can, after all."

"You'd be surprised," smiled Mr. Wells.

As there were no other customers in the store just then and he had plenty of time, he got a pencil and paper and began to show the boys what he meant.

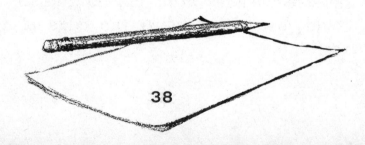

First he drew squares on the paper, like this.

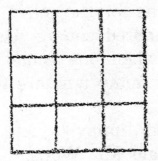

"Now," he began, "suppose each of those squares is one foot wide and one foot long. That is what we call one square foot."

The boys leaned over the counter to watch. It was easy enough to understand, so far.

"Now here," Mr. Wells went on, "we've got three and three and three, which make nine. Nine square feet. Or you can put it this way."

He drew the squares again, like this.

"It doesn't matter which way you put them," he said, "as long as you have nine squares. It takes just as much paint for the one as for the other. You'll see that one hundred square feet is not so very much when you come to measure it out. How many tens are there in one hundred?"

"Ten," said Jimmy.

"Right," said Mr. Wells.

This time he measured his squares right on the floor.

40

"Ten feet long and ten feet wide," said Mr. Wells, "is just one hundred square feet. You count it up. You can see for yourselves just how big it looks."

The boys counted. Mr. Wells was right. It did not seem big at all. They were surprised.

"Now, what you have to do," said Mr. Wells, "is to find out how many square feet there are on each side of your shed."

"Do you mean we have to count it all off in squares?" Bill asked. That seemed like too much work.

Mr. Wells laughed.

"You needn't do all that," he said. "These squares were just to show you what I mean. All you need do is to measure how long each side is and how high it is. Then I'll do the work, and I'll tell you how much paint you want. And if I'm right about that shed," he added, "one big can of paint will just about do the whole thing."

The girls waited at the store while the boys went back and measured the shed. The sides were easy. The two ends were a bit harder because they ran up into a point under the roof. The boys didn't know just what to do about that. At last they got a box to stand on, and Bill measured from the top of the point down to the ground, using a stick where he could not reach and measuring the stick when he was through. That was near enough. They wrote their measures down and took them back to Mr. Wells.

Mr. Wells worked them out. Counting the two ends and the two sides, it came to a little over four hundred square feet.

The boys couldn't believe it. One can of paint wouldn't be nearly enough!

"I think it will," said Mr. Wells. "One big can is supposed to do three hundred square feet, using two coats of paint. That's what it says on the can. Most barns and houses need two coats of paint, so the paint makers always count on that. But I think one coat of paint will do on your shed for one summer. So you will have enough to paint it all over once, and maybe a little left over for the inside."

He took down one of his big cans of paint and set it on the counter.

"There you are," he said. "Now, wait a minute. You need other things. Have you got a paintbrush?"

They had no paintbrush, so Mr. Wells took a brush and laid it beside the paint can.

"You need drier and oil, too," he went on, "to put with your paint. That paint is too thick to use the way it is now. You need to thin it out, and then it will make more. What's the matter? Does painting sound like hard work?"

The boys were beginning to look worried. All these things cost money, and they had only half a dollar. Someone had to tell Mr. Wells.

At last Jimmy explained.

"You see, Mr. Wells, it's like this. We haven't enough money to buy all these things right now. We just thought we'd find out what they cost, and then maybe we could earn enough money to pay for them."

Mr. Wells said, "Well, suppose first of all we just add up what everything comes to. That's what we call making out a bill. Now, is there anything else you need?"

"There's the inside," said Bill. "We'd like to fix the inside, too."

And Jimmy added, "We thought of wallpaper. Ann wanted wallpaper."

"With roses on it," put in Ann.

Mr. Wells tapped his nose with his pencil. He was thinking.

"I've got some wallpaper," he said, "that was left over from last year. It has roses on it, and I think it is just the kind of paper you would like, Ann. There are only two rolls left, but I guess two rolls will be enough for you. And you can have it for ten cents a roll. That's less than it cost me, but I know Ann wants it."

He began to make out his bill.

"You'd better have two brushes," he said, "because, if I know you boys, you'll both want to be painting at the same time, and one brush won't be enough. Now let's see."

The bill was like this.

1 can paint	$1.50
oil	.30
drier	.40
2 brushes	.70
wallpaper	.20
	$3.10

When Bill saw it, he whistled. Jimmy said, "Three dollars and ten cents! I guess it will take all summer to earn that much money!"

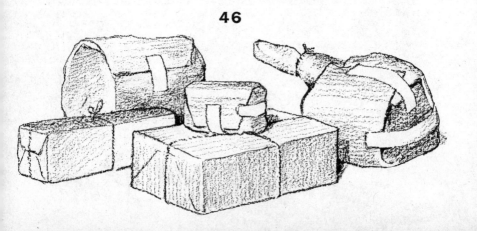

"Oh, no, it won't," said Mr. Wells. "I tell you what we can do about it. I am pretty busy these days. If I don't have to take my truck out for short trips, it will save me some time. You don't need a truck just to carry round a new broom or a can of paint. Now, if you boys want to carry packages for me, for two hours every afternoon, I'll pay you each twenty-five cents a day. In that way, it won't take you very long to work off your bill. What do you think about it?"

The boys thought the idea was fine.

"Then in about a week we'll be able to have our paint," Bill cried.

"You can have your paint now," said Mr. Wells. "Everyone has to take chances sometimes. I'll take my chance that you boys will keep your promise about working for me. I'm pretty sure that if you say you will work that bill off, you are going to do it."

Great Changes

The mothers were very much pleased about the Five-and-a-Half Club. They were pleased with anything that would keep the children happy and busy all day. Now, maybe, there would be a little quiet and comfort about the house.

That evening Mrs. Baker was even more pleased. Jimmy and Ann washed their hands for supper without being reminded, and Ann hurried to get the table all set and the chairs put around, ten full minutes before suppertime.

"Well, this is nice!" said Mrs. Baker to herself.

Nearly always, when Ann set the table, she forgot something — the glasses or the bread or the knives. But this time not one thing was missing. It was wonderful! And after supper, while Ann carried the china to the kitchen, Jimmy asked,

"Don't you want me to dry the dishes for you, Mother?"

Now, ever since Jimmy had had measles last spring, he seemed to think that he had to be very careful not to get tired out. Playing didn't tire him, of course, but doing things around the house did, and most of all, drying dishes. Right after dinner or supper was the time Jimmy always began to feel bad.

His mother looked at him.

"That would be very nice of you," she said, "but I don't want you to get all tired out. You've been outdoors all day. Maybe you'd better take a book and lie down for a little while."

"But I'd like to help you," Jimmy said. "I'd love to dry the dishes if you'll let me."

"Oh, I'll let you," said Mrs. Baker.

So Jimmy got one dish towel and Ann got another, and between them they dried so fast that their mother could hardly keep up with them. The dishwashing was over in no time at all; and when the towels were hung up and everything put away, Jimmy said,

"I'll brush up the floor, too, if you like."

And Ann said, "Don't you want me to water the flowers, Mother?"

This time Mrs. Baker looked at both of them, very hard. She felt a little worried. Jimmy was so good and quiet, and Ann's face looked a little hot. They both seemed to act so strange, as if they were not feeling well.

And then Jimmy said, "Mother —"
and Ann began, "Mother — " and they
both stopped short.

"What is the matter?" asked poor Mrs.
Baker.

Ann began again, "We were just
wondering — "

Jimmy said, "We don't want to trouble
you or anything, Mother. But you know
that old cane-seated chair up in the storeroom, and the little stool? We were
thinking if you didn't want them any
more, maybe we could have them for our
clubhouse."

"So that's it," said their mother, and she began to laugh. "Well, you can have the chair, and you can have the stool," she said. "But the next time you want anything, you'd better come right out and ask for it and not try to put me off the track by all this talk of drying dishes and watering flowers!"

Over at the Strong house it was the same way. Only when Bill and Martha started being helpful, their mother saw through it at once. She knew that children didn't act like that without a reason. So when Bill started to empty the paper basket and brush up the floor, she said,

"You put that broom down, Bill Strong. And Martha, you stop fiddling with those dishes. Now tell me just what it is you want, because I know very well you want something!"

And then it all came out. They wanted anything that Mother could give them to help fix up the clubhouse.

Next day there was a great "to-do" in the Baker house and in the Strong house. Every minute Jimmy or Ann or Bill or Martha came running to ask, "Can we have this? Can we have that?"

It was as good as a spring house cleaning.

When they came to count up, there were a good many things. There were the chair and stool from the Baker storeroom, and a blue glass dish. There were an old rug and a candlestick. There were a little table that needed to have one leg mended, and a painted bench, and a number of other things that the children thought might be useful.

All in all, the Five-and-a-Half Club was doing very well.

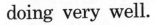

Painting House

Painting was fun, Bill thought. When he was older, he would earn money painting houses for people. He slapped his brush up and down as far as he could reach, and each slap left a long, shiny streak of red paint.

By afternoon the boys had the whole front of the shed painted. Sally and Ann and Martha wanted to paint, too, but the boys would not let them.

"House painting is man's work," Bill said. "Maybe you can paint the door on the inside — if there's any paint left over," he added with some doubt. He looked down at the paint can. The paint seemed to be getting used up pretty fast. Maybe it needed more thinning.

"We'll finish this end where it shows most," Jimmy said. "Then when we get around to the back, we can thin it out more."

"You'd better start thinning it right now," Sally told him, "or else you won't have enough to go round."

"Girls always think they know better than anyone else," Bill said.

Sally was quite sure that she knew. She had helped her grandmother paint the kitchen last summer.

After a while Jimmy cried out, "See! I guess Sally was right after all! Look at that. We're going to need another half can of paint before we are through. That means working two more days for Mr. Wells."

"Don't forget the weeding, either," cried Ann. "Those weeds are starting to come up pretty fast."

It was true. Ann and Sally walked over to look. Weeds were already showing between the rows. This evening Mr. Riley would be sure to look at his garden.

"Let's work on it now," Sally said. "Then, when the boys get through painting, they can do their share to make up."

Down they went on their hands and knees and set to work, up one row and down the other. It was surprising how many weeds there were when they got them all pulled out and piled together.

This was only the beginning of weeding for Ann and Sally. What with painting the shed and working two hours a day for Mr. Wells, the boys never seemed to get time for weeding. Sally and Ann did most of it. Martha helped them. Martha did not always know the difference between weeds and garden plants, so Sally was afraid to let her do much pulling up, but she could rake and pile.

Little redheaded Bobby Wells helped, too. When Bobby's mother was busy, she was glad to let Bobby come over and play with the older boys and girls, as long as Sally would look after him. Bobby liked to work. He brought his wagon and his rake and helped Martha.

But there were other things Bobby liked better than weeding. He liked watching Jimmy and Bill paint. He felt sure that he could paint, too, if only the boys would let him. He didn't want to spend all his time just helping the girls.

Paste Is Made to Stick

One afternoon Bobby wandered over to the clubhouse by himself. There was no one around. Sally was helping to clean house at home. The two boys were working for Mr. Wells. Martha and Ann were at Ann's house.

Bobby touched the shed wall with his hand. It felt nice and dry. He pulled up a weed stalk and made believe it was a paintbrush, slapping it up and down the way he had seen Bill do. While he painted, he talked.

"Here comes my big paintbrush! Hello, you old Mr. Spider. You'd better watch out! If you don't hurry, I'm going to paint right over you!"

The spider did hurry. The weed stalk broke, and Bobby threw it away. It wasn't much fun painting without real paint. He went inside the shed.

That morning Bill and Jimmy and Sally had hung the first pieces of wallpaper. It was quite a job. They had papered all one end and part of the side wall, and then they had had to stop for dinner. They were in a hurry, so they had left everything just as it was.

There stood the pail of paste, which Mrs. Green had made for them, and there were two pieces of wallpaper already cut.

All that morning Bobby had watched the others work. It looked easy. First they laid the paper on a board, wrong side up, and pasted it all over. Then Bill stood on a chair and held the top end of the paper straight against the wall while Sally and Jimmy patted it down smooth and flat.

All morning Bobby had longed to get hold of that paste brush. He had pasted pictures in his book at home. He was sure he could paste wallpaper. Now, if he could only get those two pieces of paper pasted nicely on the wall, it would be a grand surprise for the others when they got back. They would say, "Why, just look what Bobby did, all by himself!" After that, Bobby thought, they would know that he really was big enough to do things. Then they would let him help instead of just stand round looking on.

He dipped the big brush into the paste and set to work. He spread paste all over the paper the way he had seen Sally do — slap, slap. It was easy. He was careful to use lots and lots of paste so that the paper would stick.

When he had the paper pasted and ready, Bobby pulled his chair near the wall and put a box on the chair so that he could reach way up. By standing on tiptoe, he got the top edge of his paper stuck to the wall. That was fine.

But now the trouble began. The paper was wet and heavy with all the paste Bobby had spread on it. And there was nearly as much paste on Bobby's hands as there was on the paper. Instead of sticking to the wall, the paper stuck to Bobby. It stuck fast. Each time he got it off from one part of him, it stuck somewhere else.

Now Bobby was getting angry. He gave a big pull to get away. And what a surprise he got! The top part of the paper that he had put up so carefully pulled away from the wall and fell right down over his head like a wet, heavy blanket. It was wetter than the tent in the back yard had ever been.

Sally was working in her kitchen. She heard a bump and a loud call. In a minute she was out the back door and across to the clubhouse.

An overturned chair and a big ball of wet, sticky wallpaper were all that she could see. But the yells that she had heard at home were now louder. They seemed to be coming right out from the middle of the wallpaper ball that was rolling and tossing around on the floor.

65

Sally started pulling at the paper. Soon two arms were waving in the air. Two kicking legs came next, and then a funny face, wet and sticky from tears and paste. It was Bobby. But what a sight he was! He was paste from head to foot, and bits of wet wallpaper were sticking to him all over. Sally had to laugh, and the more she laughed the more angry Bobby got. The noise he made was louder than even Mr. Riley had ever dreamed of.

Ann and Martha came running from across the road. Together they got Bobby over to Sally's kitchen. While the children filled a tub with water, Mrs. Green pulled off Bobby's shoes and sun suit. In less than no time he was in the tub.

"Run over to Bobby's house, Ann," Mrs. Green said, "and get some dry clothes for him. Tell his mother that I'll wash out this suit and hang it up here."

Then she set to work on Bobby. Getting his hair clean was hardest. Mrs. Green had made that paste good and strong. There was nothing to do but use cold water. Splash! splash! went the water on Bobby's head. With every splash he shivered from cold and excitement. But he did not cry or yell. There was no time for that now. Mrs. Green's hands fairly flew, and soon Bobby heard the welcome words, "There, I guess you'll do."

Another few minutes and Bobby was sitting at the kitchen table, dressed in clean, dry clothes. And there were Mrs. Green, Ann, and Sally standing around him. It was good to see again! Sally had brought the cooky jar and some milk, so they could have milk and cookies all round.

"Goodness, he looked funny," said Sally, "all rolled up in a ball!"

"I guess you'd look funny, too, if you had wallpaper all over you," said her grandmother. "We're lucky it wasn't paint. You can't get paint off with plain cold water."

Suddenly Bobby laid down his cooky and started to cry.

"I wanted to help! I wanted to have a nice surprise for you. Now the paper's all spoiled, and it won't be a surprise any more!"

"Never you mind, Bobby," Sally said. She gave him a big hug. "Tomorrow you can help us. If you put the paste on the paper, Bill and I can hang it much faster. We'll let you be the paste man. Won't that be fine?"

Bobby stopped crying. He smiled all over his face. Now he really would be one of the boys!

Mr. Bunson

Bill and Jimmy liked working for Mr. Wells. Working for other people is always more fun than working at home. Raking the yard or running to the store for a loaf of bread was no fun. But carrying packages round for Mr. Wells was all right.

When there were no packages to carry, Mr. Wells let the boys help him in the store. They sorted nails and put things straight on the shelves. Sometimes they waited on people, too. They felt important to be selling can openers or pie tins and doing up packages.

One afternoon Mrs. Brooks came into the store. Bill and Jimmy liked Mrs. Brooks. Two years ago, before she became Mr. Brooks's wife, she had been their teacher in school.

Mrs. Brooks bought a new broom and some clothesline and a can of green paint. She wanted the things sent round that afternoon. Bill and Jimmy were glad to take them.

When the boys got to Mrs. Brooks's house, they tapped at the front door. No one came. They went round to the kitchen door. No one was in the kitchen, either.

Then all at once they saw Mrs. Brooks. She was out in her back garden. She was crawling on her hands and knees between the beans and the currant bushes. All they could see at first was just her head.

Bill said, "I wonder what she's doing."

"Looks as if she's playing at something," said Jimmy.

It did look that way. First Mrs. Brooks would crawl slowly, and then she would make a sudden jump. Then she would look all around her, and after that she would begin crawling again.

Bill said, "You don't suppose she's gone crazy, do you?"

Bill had read a book once which told about travelers in the desert who went crazy from too much sun. But there was not so much sun today. Besides, the boys had talked to Mrs. Brooks in the store not half an hour ago. She seemed all right then.

Just then Mrs. Brooks caught sight of the two boys. She said, "Sh-h. Come over here quickly and don't make any noise."

The boys went on tiptoe between the bushes. They looked where Mrs. Brooks was pointing.

Away across the garden, by the fence, they saw a white rabbit. He was moving very slowly — clop, clop — and every few clops he would stop to bite off the top of one of Mrs. Brooks's flowers. His ears twitched and his nose twitched, and all the while he kept one eye on Mrs. Brooks. When she moved, he moved. When she stopped, he stopped, too.

Mrs. Brooks said, "I don't know where he came from, but he's eating up all my garden. You boys crawl round the garden, one on each side, and maybe we can catch him."

The boys started off, Jimmy on one side and Bill on the other. But the rabbit was wise. He had been chased before. He waited until they were close to him, and then off he went again. Up one row and down the other they chased him until they were hot and tired.

"He's worse than a frog," said Bill.

Jimmy called out to the rabbit, "You wait a minute. I'll fix you, pretty quick!"

He brought an empty fruit basket from Mrs. Brooks's back steps.

"You chase him until he gets in a corner," he said to Bill. "Then I'll drop the basket over him. Go easy, and don't get him too frightened."

This time it was Mrs. Brooks and Bill who did the chasing, while Jimmy stood and waited. Over and over again they got the rabbit right up to the fence corner, and each time Jimmy made a jump with his basket, and missed. At last there came a shout from Jimmy, "I've got him!"

"Good work!" said Mrs. Brooks. "The question is, what shall we do with him? We can't let him go again. He'd only go and eat up someone else's garden."

"Maybe he belongs to someone," Bill said, "and just got out by mistake."

The boys looked through the slats of the basket. The rabbit looked right back at them. Now that he was safely caught, he didn't seem wild at all. He acted just as any tame rabbit would.

Jimmy poked a finger through the slats, and the rabbit smelled at it.

"He's still hungry," said Jimmy. "If we let him out, he'll start eating all over again."

"Not in my garden!" laughed Mrs. Brooks. "Now you have him, and you can keep him. But you'd better find out first whether he belongs to anyone round here. If he does, you will have to give him back."

"We'll ask Mr. Wells," said Bill. "Maybe he will know."

Mrs. Brooks gave the boys a cloth to tie over the basket, and they carried the rabbit back to the store until it was time to go home.

"I don't know of anyone around here who has white rabbits," said Mr. Wells. "Mr. Best has rabbits, but his rabbits are all brown. Maybe this one came from a long way off. I'll tell you what you do. Put up a notice in the post office. Then if someone in town did lose a white rabbit, he will know where to find him."

The next day a notice was put up in the post office. It read:

FOUND!
A WHITE RABBIT
IN MRS. BROOKS'S
GARDEN.
WILL THE OWNER
PLEASE CALL

JIMMY BAKER
OR
BILL STRONG

Meantime, the boys fixed up a nice rabbit pen, made of wooden boxes and netting. It filled nearly one whole end of the clubhouse.

Every day Ann or Martha or Sally would say, "I do hope no one asks for our rabbit!" Bill and Jimmy said nothing. They just waited.

For ten days the notice hung in the post office. Then the boys took it down. The white rabbit was theirs.

The rabbit seemed to like his new home. While he was running wild, he had to hunt for his dinner. Now his dinner was brought to him. He was a friendly rabbit, too, with plenty of good sense. Soon he grew very tame. The children named him Mr. Bunson.

Bobby loved Mr. Bunson. He brought him food every day.

The only person who did not like Mr. Bunson was old Mr. Riley. Mr. Riley wasn't sure about rabbits, even in pens. They might get out, and then what would happen to his garden?

He said, "You'd better watch that rabbit. Once he gets out, there'll be an end of him and an end of your playhouse, too!"

"He won't get out," Sally said.

"He'd better not," said Mr. Riley.

Secrets

The Five-and-a-Half Club wanted to give a party. It was to be a birthday party. Mrs. Strong and Mrs. Baker both had a birthday on the same day. That would be a grand day to give the party and ask all the mothers to come. There would be four mothers, counting Mrs. Green, who was really a grandmother, but that was the same thing. Four was just the right number. Two of the mothers could have chairs, and the other two could sit on the bench.

"It's a good thing we haven't all got different mothers," said Ann. "Four is about all that will fit in."

"Three could sit on the bench if they sat close," said Sally. "And there's the stool, too. I think," she went on, "that we should ask Mr. Riley, as well."

"Mr. Riley isn't a mother," said Ann.

"It's his shed," said Sally. "We've never asked him to come and see it since it was all fixed up. This would be a good chance."

"I guess he's seen it already," Jimmy broke in. "He was looking around here the other day. I expect he likes to know what we are doing."

"We should ask Mrs. Riley, anyway," Sally insisted.

No one had thought about Mrs. Riley. No one knew Mrs. Riley very well. She spent nearly all the time in her own house.

Bill said, "I say that we should just stick to our own mothers. Once we ask Mrs. Riley, we'll have to ask other people, too. There won't be enough places to sit. And there won't be enough cookies, either."

As the boys had promised to buy the cookies, there was nothing more to be said. Ever since Bill and Jimmy had worked for Mr. Wells, they had been giving themselves airs. They liked to be important. When the club first talked about giving a party, Bill had said,

"Don't you worry about the cookies. We'll see to all that. All you girls need to do is to bring teacups and make the tea."

All the same, Sally secretly made up her mind to ask Mrs. Riley. It would be only right. If there were not enough cookies to go round, she could go without, herself. She wouldn't mind — much. Mrs. Riley was an old lady. Old ladies didn't eat much, anyway, but they liked tea. Maybe Mrs. Riley wouldn't come. She hardly ever went anywhere, but it would please her to be asked. Bill and Jimmy need not think that they could run everything their own way. If they could have their secrets, Sally could have hers, too. She would write a note to Mrs. Riley that very night.

Ann and Martha had a secret, too. Each wanted to think of some nice birthday gift for her mother. The girls didn't want to buy their gifts. They wanted to make them. Made gifts are always nicer. Ann thought that she would make a kettle holder. Her mother had been needing a new kettle holder for a long time. Only yesterday she had said, "I really must remember to get a new kettle holder."

Martha thought that she would make her mother a bag, a little bag with strings, to keep buttons in.

Over at Martha's house Mrs. Strong was busy cutting out new dresses — two for Martha and one for herself. She had just got her own dress all cut out when the fruit man came to the back door. Martha's mother dropped her work and went out into the kitchen to talk to him.

It was just then that Martha and Ann came into the house. They were looking for something they could use to make their gifts.

There were plenty of pieces of cloth around. There were bits of white with blue spots and bits of brown with white spots left over from Martha's new dresses. But Ann and Martha didn't want spots. They wanted something prettier.

All at once Martha saw something under the table. There, on the floor, were two pieces that would do splendidly. They were odd-shaped bits, just big enough to make a little bag and a kettle holder, and they were of a most beautiful blue with little white flowers all over. They were pieces of dress goods that Martha's mother had been cutting out for her own new dress.

Ann and Martha were delighted. Had they searched high and low, they could not have found anything prettier.

Ann asked, "Do you suppose it's all right if we take them?"

Martha was sure that it would be all right. When Mother was cutting out, she always dropped the leftover bits she did not want right on the floor, to be picked up later. The big pieces that she did want she rolled up into a bundle. But anything that Martha found on the floor she could always take to make doll clothes. She didn't even have to ask.

The two little girls hurried out. Their sewing was to be very, very secret. They were going to do it over at the clubhouse.

It took Martha's mother some time to buy her apples and potatoes. When she had finished and had returned to the living room, she looked at the clock. Half past twelve and nearly time for dinner! First she must put her sewing things away and then call Martha to come and set the table.

She gathered up all her pieces of cloth just as they were and put them into a big, flat box. There the pieces would be quite safe until she was ready to sew them together.

Where Are My Sleeves?

It was not until three days later that Mrs. Strong had time to settle down to her dressmaking again. Martha and Ann were over at the clubhouse. Bill was out with Jimmy. The house was nice and quiet. Mrs. Strong thought that she would have a good long afternoon to sew on her new dress.

She got out the flat box with all her sewing in it, that she had put away so carefully, and set to work. She laid out the pieces for her dress. But when she came to look for the two sleeves, she could not find them anywhere. She looked all through the box, but her two sleeves were not there.

"That's a queer thing," said Mrs. Strong to herself.

She searched through the box again. Then she took all the cutout pieces of dress goods and shook them. She laid them on the table and counted them again. Everything else was there, but not the two sleeves.

"Now I know," said Mrs. Strong, "that I cut those sleeves out!"

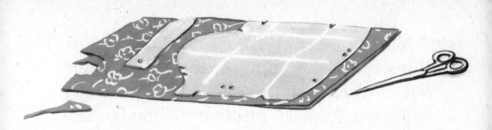

She was quite sure about it. She remembered very well, indeed, because it was just then that the fruit man had come to the back door. She had left everything on the table; and when she came back, she had gathered all her sewing together and had put it away.

"They must be somewhere," said Mrs. Strong to herself. She searched again.

Where on earth could those two sleeves have gone?

At suppertime Mrs. Strong was still worrying about her sleeves. After supper she searched all through the box once more, in case she had made a mistake. She searched all over the room.

"I don't suppose," she said to Martha, "that you have seen two cutout sleeves lying about anywhere, have you?"

Martha replied, "No, Mother, I haven't."

Martha said it before she stopped to think; but the minute the words were out of her mouth, she had an empty feeling right down inside her. She remembered those odd-shaped blue pieces that she and Ann had picked up off the floor. Could they have been Mother's two sleeves? Suddenly she knew, just as well as if someone were saying it out loud. She could feel her face grow hot and red. But luckily her mother was too busy to notice.

"Well, I'll just have to give it up," Mrs. Strong said. "It will mean buying another half yard of goods, and I don't even know that I can get it. I bought the goods down at Singer's store, and it was about the last yard of it that they had. Mr. Singer said he didn't know whether he could get any more or not."

"You will have to make your dress without any sleeves," said Martha's father. "It will be nice and cool for the hot weather!"

Mr. Strong always liked a joke. But this was one time when Martha's mother didn't feel like joking. Instead, she answered crossly,

"Of course I can't go round in a dress without any sleeves! No one has dresses without sleeves this year!"

Martha could stand no more. She slipped quietly out of the room and up to her own little bedroom to think. Something had to be done. But what should it be?

Early next morning she ran over to Ann's house to tell her what had happened. Ann felt every bit as bad as Martha. Neither of them knew what to do. If only they had not been in such a hurry to get their gifts cut out and started! But there were the two sleeves, all cut up to make a bag and a kettle holder! Mrs. Strong couldn't go round all summer with a kettle holder on one arm and a bag on the other.

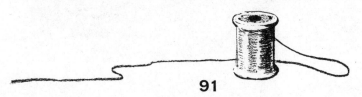

"I tell you what we'll do," said Ann. "We'll put our money together, and we'll go down to Singer's and buy her another piece."

"But suppose they don't have any more?"

"We can find out, anyway," Ann said.

Martha had twenty-five cents. Ann had only twenty. Ann had been saving up to buy flowers for her mother's birthday. Martha needed ribbon for her bag, and the ribbon cost ten cents a yard. Now maybe she would have to do without ribbon.

Singer's was the big store right at the other end of Main Street, past the post office and the bank and the railroad station. It was a long way. Their mothers nearly always took the bus when they went shopping at Singer's. Ann and Martha had no money for the bus. They would have to walk all the way there and back.

Ann and Martha had never been downtown all alone. They felt a little frightened as they started out. When they went downtown in the bus with their mothers, it seemed to take only a minute. Now it seemed as if the sidewalk stretched on and on forever.

They passed the school and the new firehouse. They passed Mrs. Brooks's house. Mrs. Brooks was out in her front garden. When she saw the girls, she came down to the fence to ask how the white rabbit was getting on. Ann and Martha stayed so long talking to Mrs. Brooks that they had to hurry to make up for lost time.

By the time they got to Main Street, they were all out of breath.

On Main Street it is not easy to hurry. There are too many people — people with baby carts, people doing their marketing or else just stopping to look in at the store windows. Today there were two women who walked ever so slowly right in front of Ann and Martha all the way from the bank to the Five-and-Ten. Whenever Ann or Martha tried to pass them on one side, the women moved to that side, too. At last they stopped to look in at the Five-and-Ten windows so that Ann and Martha could get by.

The two little girls were afraid every minute that they would meet someone they knew, someone who would ask them what they were doing downtown all by themselves. They stepped as fast as they could and hoped that no one would see them.

When they got to Singer's, just inside
the doorway, Ann gave Martha's skirt a
little pull. She whispered, "There's Mrs.
Wells, buying shoes for Bobby. Let's go
round the other way."

The shoe department at Singer's was
like a room all by itself, near the door.
Mrs. Wells was sitting with her back
turned, trying shoes on Bobby. All they
could see was her hat and the back of
Bobby's red head.

Martha and Ann tiptoed past Mrs. Wells very softly. They made their way past the long table with the piles of skirts and blouses on it, right to the back of the store. There they were safe, even if Mrs. Wells turned her head.

"Let's just be looking round," Ann said.

They looked at everything in turn. They looked at aprons and stockings and babies' coats. They looked at the dress goods, too, but they did not see anything that looked like Martha's mother's dress.

Everyone seemed busy. There was a woman buying stockings and another woman buying towels. There were two of the Singer young ladies busy talking to each other behind the dress counter. No one took any notice of Ann and Martha. No one asked them what they wanted. Little girls often looked around by themselves in Singer's store while their mothers were busy shopping.

By and by Martha went back to look at the place where they sold shoes. Mrs. Wells and Bobby had gone, she said, when she came back.

It was Ann who went up to the counter and said to one of the young ladies in her best grown-up voice, "Will you wait on us, please? We want to buy some dress goods."

"What kind of dress goods?" asked the young lady, with a smile.

"It's a blue kind," Ann said, "with little white flowers on it."

"Did you bring a little bit of the goods with you?"

Ann and Martha looked at each other. They hadn't thought about matching the goods.

"I guess we forgot to," said Ann.

The young lady was very kind. She took down roll after roll of blue goods, all the rolls there were on the shelf. The little girls looked at each in turn, but not one of the rolls was the right kind.

"Are you sure it came from this store?" the young lady asked them.

"I know it did," said Martha. "Mother said so. And she said you didn't have very much of it, only just enough for her dress. But we thought — "

"Oh," said the young lady. Then she called, "Mr. Singer! Will you please come here for a minute?"

Mr. Singer came over. He was short and fat, and he wore gold eyeglasses. He smiled at Ann and Martha.

"Mr. Singer," asked the young lady, "do you know whether we have that new lot of dress goods in yet, like the kind we had last week?"

"Yes," said Mr. Singer, "it came in this morning, but it is not unpacked yet. I could let you have it by this afternoon."

Ann and Martha could not wait until afternoon. They wanted it now.

Mr. Singer seemed to understand. "I'll see what I can do," he said.

And off he went.

He was gone a long time, Martha and Ann thought. They waited and waited. Once Ann said that she guessed Mr. Singer must be having a lot of trouble finding that dress goods. The young lady smiled. "He doesn't mind," she said. "He is glad to help people."

At last Mr. Singer came back, out of breath and looking hot. He was carrying three big, heavy rolls, all done up in brown paper. They made a bang when he dropped them on the counter.

Mr. Singer blew his breath out as he said, "Now we'll see!"

Martha and Ann could hardly wait.

Mr. Singer undid a bit of paper from the first roll so that they could see inside.

The roll of dress goods was green.

He undid some from the second roll. This roll was just like Martha's mother's dress, only it was red instead of blue.

Then Mr. Singer undid the last roll of all.

"That's it!" Martha cried. "That's it!"

"Are you quite sure?" Mr. Singer asked.

Martha was very sure. So was Ann.

Off came the rest of the paper, and there was the blue goods, a whole new roll of it, just the same as Martha's mother's dress. Yard after yard of it soon lay in a big pile on the counter.

"Now," he said, "how many yards would you little ladies like?"

Ann said, "We just want half a yard, please."

"How much?" asked Mr. Singer, as if he had not heard right.

"Half a yard, please," said Ann again.

Mr. Singer looked at the young lady. The young lady looked at Mr. Singer. And they both began to laugh. Neither Ann nor Martha could see why. Then the young lady measured just half a yard. She cut it off and put it into a paper bag. "Twenty-five cents," she said, as she handed the bag to Ann.

"That was lucky," said Ann.

The two little girls stood on the sidewalk outside Singer's store, counting up their money. Martha still had to buy her ribbon.

"That will be ten," she said, "and we'll have ten cents left over. We could take the bus back," she added, thinking of that long walk home.

But Ann thought that it would be better to spend their money on ice-cream cones; and as soon as she said it, Martha thought so, too.

They bought Martha's ribbon. They ate their ice-cream cones, sitting on high stools at the Five-and-Ten counter. Then they started back.

Before they had gone far, who should overtake them but Mrs. Wells, driving back with Bobby in her car.

"Don't you want a lift?" Mrs. Wells called.

So they hopped into the car, and Mrs. Wells drove them all the way home. She never once asked them what they had been doing downtown all by themselves! Maybe she knew about the birthdays.

Next day Mrs. Strong opened the box where she kept her sewing. She was not looking for her sleeves this time because she knew quite well that they were not there. She had searched through that box five times already. Today it was thread she needed to sew a torn apron.

When she opened the box, there, right at the bottom, was a big new piece of blue goods like her dress. She couldn't believe her eyes. How did it get there?

"It can't be," she said to herself, "that I never cut those sleeves out after all. Why, I know I cut them out!"

And then she caught sight of a little bit of paper that had fallen out. It was a bill from Singer's store, and it said,

Half yard dress goods............25

"Hum," said Mrs. Strong. "So that's it, is it?"

But she was like Mrs. Wells. She didn't ask any questions.

The Birthday Party

On the day of the party it seemed as if four o'clock would never come. All morning Ann and Sally and Martha had been fixing up the clubhouse. Flowers were on the table and teacups all set out. The teacups had come from Mrs. Green's house. Everything looked very nice, the girls thought.

The boys had their own surprise for the party. It was hidden away in Mrs. Green's icebox. Only Mrs. Green knew what it was, and she had promised not to tell.

At four o'clock the mothers arrived. They were surprised to see how nice the clubhouse looked. Mrs. Wells said that she would like to move right in and live there herself. Mrs. Baker looked at the walls. "I declare," she said, "I'll give you boys the job of painting my back kitchen next time!"

Bobby was the most excited of all. He kept hopping up and down, asking everyone to look at the wallpaper he had helped to paste.

First the girls handed around tea and cookies. Then the boys brought in their surprise.

It was ice cream!

Mrs. Baker said, "I haven't been to such a nice party for years!"

She was sitting next to Mrs. Strong on the bench, with a cup in one hand and a cooky in the other. Mrs. Green and Mrs. Wells had the two chairs. The boys and girls sat on the floor.

Jimmy said, "This place is as full as an egg! I guess if we tried to get one more person in here, the walls would pop out!"

And just as he said it, one more person arrived. It was Mrs. Riley.

No one but Sally knew that Mrs. Riley had been asked to the party. She came across the garden in her best dress with a white apron tied over it, and she was carrying a big cake with chocolate icing on it!

"I guess I'm a bit late for the party," Mrs. Riley said. "I would have been here sooner, but I was waiting for the icing to set. As long as I was asked to the party, I wanted to bring something along with me."

Bill and Jimmy looked at each other. They were thinking of the mean things they had said when Sally spoke of asking Mrs. Riley to the party. Even their ears felt red. But no one was taking any notice of them. Everyone was looking at Mrs. Riley's cake.

It had chocolate icing all over, and on top of the icing in white letters were the words HAPPY BIRTHDAY. Did anyone ever have a grander cake?

Mrs. Riley wouldn't have any tea. She said that she took tea only at suppertime. But she would like a cooky, she said, as she sat down on Mrs. Wells's chair. Mrs. Wells had slipped quietly to a seat on the floor, making a "sh" sound with her lips to Martha as she did so.

And then the party began all over again.

Now it was time for the birthday gifts.

Bill's gift to his mother was a new can opener. Jimmy's was an egg beater with a red handle. Both came from Mr. Wells's store.

Then Ann and Martha brought out their two gifts. When Mrs. Baker opened her parcel from Ann, there was a lovely blue kettle holder, all made by hand. Mrs. Strong opened her gift. It was a little blue bag with ribbon strings.

Ann's mother cried, "Why, how lovely! Did you make that all by yourself, Ann? It's just what I wanted!"

But Martha's mother looked most surprised. She said, "What a sweet little bag! I'm going to hang it right at my bedside, where I can see it first thing in the morning. That is a nice surprise!"

Not one word was ever said about sleeves.

The Long Night

When Mrs. Wells had said that she would like to live in the clubhouse, she was just joking. But she gave Bill and Jimmy an idea, all the same. Why not take rugs and blankets over some night and sleep there?

Their mothers saw many reasons for not doing so. There were no lights in the shed. It might be cool, too. If it stormed, the boys would be sure to be frightened. Then they would come running home and wake everyone. There just wasn't any sense in the idea. When you had a good comfortable bed at home, why go and sleep in an old shed, of all places!

When they could not think of any more reasons against the plan, Mrs. Strong and Mrs. Baker said, "All right!" If the boys wanted to try it, they could. But if they didn't like it, they were not to come back home, waking everyone up in the middle of the night just because they'd changed their minds.

"And mind," said Mrs. Strong. "You can't have any candles or matches. If you go, you'll have to sleep in the dark."

Mrs. Strong thought that would settle it, but it didn't. Bill said,

"We can take a flashlight over. Flashlights are safe."

Their fathers said, "Fine. Let them go ahead and try. But no matches, and no waking anyone up in the night, or it will be just too bad."

By the time the boys had all their things ready, they looked as if they were setting out on a trip to the North Pole, instead of just across the road.

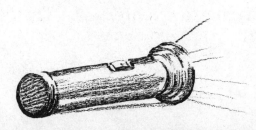

They had blankets and rugs. They had
drinking water in a milk bottle and some
cookies, in case they got hungry in the
night. A big bundle of funny papers they
had been saving up, and the flashlight,
went along, too. Jimmy had a knapsack
and Bill a big stick.

"What's the stick for?" asked Ann.

Jimmy said, "It's in case anyone comes
round trying to frighten us. That's what
it's for!"

Ann and Sally both wished that they were going to camp out in the clubhouse themselves. But they knew that they would never be allowed to. Girls never had as much fun as boys!

"I bet you'll get frightened in the night and come running home again," Ann said.

Sally laughed. She said, "Our house is the nearest. Do you want me to leave our back door open, just in case?"

"Don't you worry about us," Bill told her. "It's only girls who are afraid in the dark!"

"They aren't either. And anyway," Ann went on, "I guess I wouldn't want to go sleeping over there. There are spiders, and they'll come out at night and go walking all over you."

"Spiders aren't anything," said Jimmy. "Who cares for spiders? Besides, didn't we pull their nests down?"

It was true that they had. But not for worlds would Martha spend a night in that clubhouse. Just thinking of spiders made her crawl all over. Jimmy and Bill must be very brave to stay there all alone after dark.

Over in the clubhouse the boys made up their beds. First they laid the rugs on the floor, side by side. Then they fixed their blankets all ready to crawl into. They put the drinking water and cookies on the floor where they could be easily reached. Bill laid his stick at his bedside. They were going to be very comfortable.

There was still enough daylight to see by, as long as they kept the door open. But by the time the boys had fixed everything to their liking, it was beginning to get dark.

Jimmy stood in the doorway. He could see a light in Mrs. Green's house and a light in Mrs. Riley's kitchen, just across the garden. He could even see Mrs. Riley's shadow moving about behind the window shade. By and by the light went out. The Rileys always went to bed early.

Bill said, "Better leave the door open a crack so that we'll get some air."

Bill was already in bed. He had taken off his shoes, but he kept the rest of his clothes on. Jimmy did the same. He put his shoes at the end of his bed, as Bill had done.

The flashlight was on the floor between the two beds. It gave enough light to make the place look very comfortable. Each boy ate a cooky and took a drink of water. Then both boys lay down, pulled the blankets up, and looked at their funny papers.

"This is great," said Bill.

"It's fine," said Jimmy.

There was no one to worry them. There was no one to tell them to turn their light off. The flashlight threw long shadows up the walls. Outside they could hear cars going by on the road.

When the boys had finished reading, they put the flashlight out and lay there in the dark and talked.

The last thing Bill did was to reach out and feel for his stick at the bedside.

"That's in case anyone comes around playing jokes on us," he said.

Jimmy took a long while going to sleep. His bed had felt fine when he first lay down on it, but now it was beginning to get hard. There were bumps all over. Jimmy turned and tossed, but every way he turned things seemed to stick into him. Then he remembered that he had forgotten to empty his pockets. He reached down under the blanket and pulled out his jackknife and a mouth organ and three big nails. The bed felt better after that. He pulled his blanket up, shut his eyes tight, and soon fell asleep.

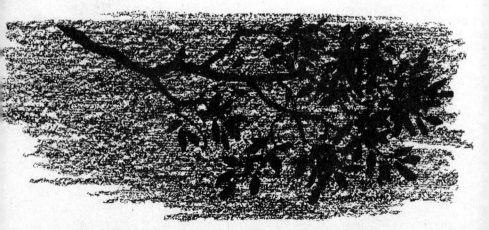

What's That?

Before long Jimmy woke up. At first he couldn't think where he was. Everything felt strange. There was no window facing his bed, where a window had always been. There was no window anywhere. Then he remembered. He was in the clubhouse. Right close to him, in the other bed, he could hear Bill breathing gently.

Jimmy listened. It was very still outside. Everything was dark. By and by he began to hear a funny thumping sound. The sound seemed to be inside of him. He found that it was his own heart, going thump-thump.

Now he could hear other noises, outside. Queer sounds, away off in the darkness — things moving around!

Bill was still asleep. Jimmy didn't see how Bill could go on sleeping with all those queer sounds going on. Jimmy waited until he couldn't stand it another minute. Then he whispered, "Bill!"

Bill never stirred. Jimmy reached over in the dark and gave him a poke. Bill woke up in a hurry. "What's the matter?" he said.

"Sh-sh," said Jimmy. "There's someone moving around."

"Where?"

"Outside. It sounds like someone walking."

"It isn't anything," said Bill, trying to sound brave.

"It is," said Jimmy. "Just you listen a minute."

The two boys listened. Now they could hear it quite plainly. "There!" said Jimmy.

Bill put the flashlight on. He held it in his hand, all ready to jump up if the sound came any nearer.

Jimmy was thinking about home. Of course, he was not afraid, but he was wondering just how long it would take, if anything did happen, to run over to his own house. He was glad that he'd gone to bed with his clothes on.

Just at that minute the flashlight went out.

Bill moved the button up and down, but there was no more light. They had used the flashlight all up reading the funny papers.

"I've got my stick, anyway," Bill said. He wasn't feeling quite so brave himself now that the light had gone out.

All at once there was a loud thump right inside the shed. Both boys jumped. Jimmy said, "Goodness! What's that?"

Now he was really frightened. He felt like running straight home.

But it was only Mr. Bunson, thumping. The boys had forgotten all about Mr. Bunson. Mr. Bunson had heard the noises, too, and he had thumped on the floor with his foot, the way rabbits always do when they hear a strange sound that they don't like. He thumped on the floor again.

Bill said, "That's just old Bun! He always does that when he gets mad. I guess there's a dog nosing round outside."

Whatever it was, the noises stopped. The boys felt better. It was not so lonely, after all, with Mr. Bunson in the shed.

"He's as good as a watchdog," Bill said. "Guess we don't have to worry, with him around!"

The boys listened a while longer. Then they pulled their blankets up and went to sleep again.

Fire!

The next time that Jimmy woke up, it was not a noise that woke him. It was a smell.

Strange noises in the dark were one thing, but a smell was another matter. A smell was real. You knew right away what it was. Jimmy knew what this was. It was the smell of smoke.

He sat up in bed, very wide awake all at once. The smell was not so strong, but it was strong enough. It wasn't inside the shed. There was nothing on fire there. It came from outside.

Jimmy went to the door. It was still dark outside, much too early for anyone to be lighting fires. The only light was the street light down the road. But the smoky smell was all around.

Jimmy went back and shook Bill. Bill was very sleepy.

"What's the matter this time? You let me alone!"

Jimmy shook him again.

"Bill, you wake up. There's something on fire some place. We've got to see what it is."

Bill rubbed his eyes. "I don't smell any — " And then he jumped right out of bed.

The smell was getting much stronger now. There was no mistake about it. Somewhere, something was on fire.

"We must wake someone up!" cried Bill.

They pulled on their shoes and ran out into the Rileys' garden. Jimmy said, "It's over there at Mr. Wells's house!"

They could make out a queer kind of light. It looked as if it were in Mr. Wells's kitchen. It kept coming and going while they looked.

The boys slipped round the back of the
shed, across Mr. Wells's garden and up
to the house, calling as they ran. Bill
banged on the back door and shook it
hard. It was locked. Jimmy ran round
to the front door, but that was locked,
too. They kept on banging and shouting,
"Mr. Wells! Mr. Wells! Your house is on
fire! There's a fire some place!"

All this time the light in the Wells's kitchen was growing stronger. The smell was getting stronger, too. It made the boys' eyes water and their noses hurt. Little clouds of smoke were coming out through the top of the kitchen window.

It seemed as if no one in that house would ever wake up!

At last Mr. Wells put his head out from an upper window. When he smelled the smoke, he didn't need to ask the boys why they were banging and shouting. He didn't say a word, but they could hear him running down the stairs.

Everyone in the house was awake now. Mr. Wells was calling up the fire department. Mrs. Wells had rolled Bobby in a blanket and had carried him out into the garden.

In another minute Mr. Wells ran to get the garden hose. Bill and Jimmy helped him. By this time the kitchen window had cracked from the heat. Mr. Wells held the hose as near the kitchen window as he could, throwing the water in through the window and up on the low kitchen roof.

Bill and Jimmy thought that they could throw pails of water on the fire from inside, too. Mr. Wells saw them start for the door. "Stay back!" he shouted. "Don't go inside."

He gave the hose to Bill. "Play it right on the roof there," he said. "And keep back. Don't you go one step nearer!"

By this time the smoke and noise had wakened everyone around — the Bakers, the Strongs, the Rileys, and the Greens.

Bill's father arrived first. "Here, fellow, give me that hose," he said. "And you stay where it's safe."

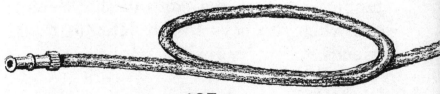

Other fathers were running in and out
of the house with Mr. Baker. Tables,
chairs, tin boxes, and pictures were
dropped on the grass. Bobby's bird was
placed under a tree with a coat thrown
over its cage. Even the Wells's cat, too
much frightened to run, was tossed right
into the middle of a flower bed, where
she landed on all four feet at once, of
course. Saving the cat was always the
funniest part of the story of the Wells's
fire when the boys told it later to their
friends.

The fire company worked fast, also. It
seemed no time at all to Bill and Jimmy
before the big truck came racing up to
the house. In a minute the firemen were
pulling out their big hose, running here
and there, and shouting to everyone to
stand back.

In less than ten minutes the fire was out. Bill and Jimmy were almost sorry when the firemen leaped onto the truck and raced away down the road. But the greatest excitement was yet to come. That was when Mr. Wells said, right in front of everyone,

"If you two boys hadn't discovered that fire in time, the whole house might have burned down!"

All at once the boys knew that what he said was true. And they knew, too, that it was sleeping in the clubhouse that had saved not only the Wells's home and maybe their own — but perhaps even the whole town. The thought made them feel very proud and brave and grown-up.

Their fathers and mothers were proud, too. They asked Mrs. Wells if there wasn't something they could do. Mrs. Wells said, "No, thank you." She was going to carry Bobby up and put him to bed again, and after that she would make them all some coffee before they went back to their own houses.

And then she laughed. But her laugh had a bit of a tear in it. She remembered that she couldn't make coffee because half her kitchen was burned out!

So, in the end, they all went over to Mrs. Green's house, which was the nearest, and Mrs. Green made coffee.

After that was over, and they had talked about the fire all over again, Mr. Strong said,

"I guess you two boys have had enough excitement by this time. You'd better come home and spend the rest of the night in your own beds."

But neither Bill nor Jimmy wanted to go home. They had started out to sleep in the clubhouse, and they were going to finish sleeping in the clubhouse. Surely there would not be anything more to waken them.

As they walked slowly back, little streaks of bright yellow-red were already in the sky. It was nearly morning.

Bill spoke first. "I bet when our families smelled the smoke and heard that old fire truck coming, they thought for sure we'd been having matches over here and set the shed on fire!"

Jimmy said, "I bet they did, too. And I guess they were surprised when they found out where the fire was. I tell you, it was a pretty lucky thing we thought of sleeping in the clubhouse tonight!"

The Wasp Nest

After the fire Bill and Jimmy went about for days feeling very proud. But feeling proud soon led them to acting proud, too, and the girls didn't like that. Martha did not mind, but Ann and Sally felt that the boys were giving themselves far too many airs. If the girls had been sleeping in the clubhouse that night, instead of the boys, wouldn't they have discovered the fire just as soon? Boys always thought that they were smarter than anyone else.

Sally and Ann felt that it was high time those boys were taken down a peg or two. Jimmy was bad enough, but Bill was worse. To hear Bill talk, one might think that he had put the whole fire out all by himself!

The girls made a secret promise to get even with Bill and Jimmy at the first chance.

There had always been a few wasps round the clubhouse. With the warm weather more and more of them arrived. Maybe they were looking for their old nests that the boys had broken down when the walls were painted.

At first the Five-and-a-Half Club did not mind them. Wasps are not likely to harm anyone if no one harms them. But with so many people in and out of the clubhouse, there was sure to be trouble. The wasps began to be spiteful. First they stung Martha and then Sally. Next, Jimmy sat down on a wasp by mistake, and he got stung. Finally, for all his smartness, Bill got stung, too, right on his ear where it hurt the most. Not being a crybaby, Bill became angry.

He said, "It's time something was done about those old wasps! Whose clubhouse is this, I want to know? Is it ours, or isn't it?"

"You can't do anything about them, except keep out of their way," Jimmy answered wisely.

"Oh, I can't, can't I!" said Bill. "We'll see." For days he went around with a stick, slapping at every wasp that he saw. This, of course, only made them more angry.

"If ever I find their nest," Bill said, "I'm going to fix them! You wait and see!"

One day Sally and Ann were walking back to Sally's house, through the fence. Right at the end of Sally's garden, in one corner, was an old apple tree. It never had any apples, so the children hardly ever went near it. But today Ann stopped all at once and pointed.

"Look," she said.

There, hanging under one of the branches, was a big, round wasp nest. It looked like a ball of gray paper. It was so much the color of the tree bark that anyone might pass it by a hundred times and never know it was there.

"I bet that's where all those wasps come from," Ann said.

She and Sally stood and looked. Then Sally went a little closer. Sally had lived in the country, so she was not quite so much afraid of wasps as Ann was.

"You look out," called Ann, getting all ready to run. "I guess there're hundreds of wasps inside. I wouldn't go poking round that nest for anything!"

Sally moved a little nearer. She looked
at the nest from all sides. She put her
ear quite close and listened. Then she
called to Ann, "Come here a minute!"

Ann didn't want to go any nearer, but she did. They both stood looking at that nest for quite a while.

Then they started to laugh.

Next day Ann said to Bill,

"Sally and I found out where the wasps' nest is."

"Where?" asked Bill. He was mending the door on Mr. Bunson's pen.

"In an old apple tree back of Sally's garden," said Ann.

"Fine," said Bill. "Now we can fix them. I'll kill every one of them. You leave it to me!"

Bill was all excited. He had the hammer in his hand, and he looked as if he were going to start out after those wasps then and there.

"You just show me where it is," he said.

The girls went ahead, and he followed, through the fence and down to the end of Sally's garden. Jimmy was not far behind.

"There," said Ann, pointing. "Hanging right on that apple-tree branch!"

Bill said, "My, that's a big one! No wonder we have wasps all around the place."

Jimmy was excited, too. He cried, "I bet there're hundreds and hundreds of them, buzzing around inside there!"

Bill went a little closer to look, and Sally called, "Watch out you don't get stung!"

Bill turned his head. He said, "I suppose you think I haven't any sense. I know what to do with wasps, all right. Don't you worry!"

"What we want to do," Bill said to Jimmy, "is to go after that nest some evening, when all the wasps are inside. Then we can catch the whole lot, all together."

"We could smoke them out," said Jimmy.

"Smoke's no good," said Bill. "I have a better idea than that. I know just what to do."

He turned to Ann and Sally.

"Now, don't you girls go fooling round that nest," he told them. "You'll only get stung. You keep right away from it, and you tell Martha and Bobby, too. I don't want anyone going near and getting those wasps all stirred up."

"We won't," said Sally.

Bill's idea did sound like a good one. All that was needed was a pail of water and a paper bag. With these things, he and Jimmy would tiptoe up and slip the bag over the wasp nest quickly and tie it tight, before the wasps had time to wake up. Then they would drop bag and nest and all into the pail of water.

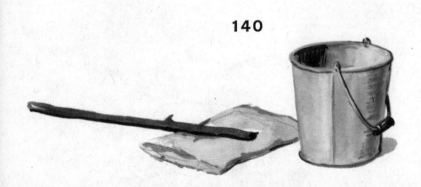

"That will kill every last wasp," Bill said.

That evening the boys got ready. First they tied thick paper around their legs. They put on coats and turned up the collars. They put on heavy mittens. Then they pulled their caps on. Last of all they dropped netting all over their heads and faces.

They were taking no chances on getting stung!

Ann and Sally and Martha gathered round to watch. Martha laughed. The boys looked so funny all bundled up, she said, as if they were going into battle.

Bill said, "That's all right. There's no sense in getting stung, is there? Now you girls had better stand way off!"

Bill and Jimmy marched up to the nest. Jimmy carried the bag and the pail, and Bill had his stick.

They moved on tiptoe. Not a sound did they make. Jimmy held the bag open, with a string round it. Slowly and carefully he slipped the bag up over the nest. Bill pulled the string tight.

"Got them!" cried Bill. "Now bring the pail, quick!" He hit the nest with his stick, and down it fell, right into the pail of water. "That's fixed them," he called to the girls. "See? Now they can't get out."

Jimmy said, "I bet they're mad, all right!"

Ann started to laugh. Then she put her hand over her mouth.

"What are you girls laughing at?" said Bill. "I guess you think it's funny, don't you?"

Ann and Sally did think that something was funny. But they never said a word. They just waited.

If those wasps were mad, they certainly
were making very little noise about it.
Not a sound came from the pail. After
a minute Jimmy said,

"You'd think we could hear them
buzzing in there. Maybe they haven't
waked up yet."

"You couldn't hear them, under the
water," Bill said. "I bet they're buzzing,
all right!"

He leaned down to listen. Then he gave the bag a poke with his stick. There wasn't a sound.

"Something queer about that," thought Bill. He wished that he knew just what those girls were laughing about, back there.

Again the boys leaned over the pail of water. Then Bill took his stick and poked around in the pail a bit harder. Sally called out, "You'd better be careful!"

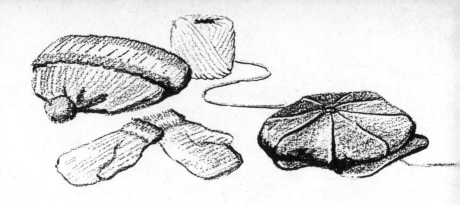

Something in Sally's voice made Bill start. What did she mean? All at once he knew. Off came netting and mittens. With bare hands he fished the wasp nest out of the water with his stick and started to break it open.

Now he knew for sure why those girls were laughing!

They had played a fine joke on him. It was just an old last year's wasp nest, and the girls had known it all along. There was not a live wasp in it. There was just one dead wasp, and it looked as if it had been dead for years and years!

Bill and Jimmy were so angry that they couldn't say a word!

Then in one voice they shouted, "All right for you! We'll get even with you someday!"

Ann and Sally ran. They ran right into Sally's kitchen and banged the door after them. The boys could hear them inside, laughing as if they were never going to stop.

The queer thing was that, after that evening, no one was ever troubled by wasps round the clubhouse again.

Sally always said that the sight of Bill and Jimmy must have frightened the live wasps so much that they all flew away and never came back!

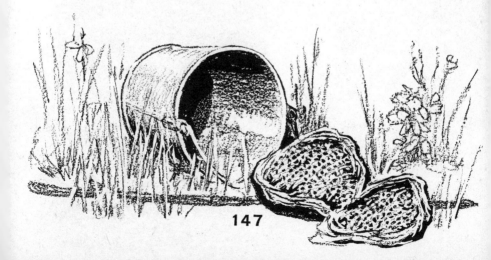

A Day in the Country

Bobby's Uncle Joe and Aunt Alice lived on a farm. As soon as they heard about the fire, they said to Mr. and Mrs. Wells, "You'd better send Bobby out to the country to stay with us. You can't cook dinners for Bobby without any kitchen to cook in."

Bobby was very glad, and Mr. and Mrs. Wells were glad, too. Ever since the fire Bobby had stayed close to the house. Watching men at work was much more exciting than belonging to the Five-and-a-Half Club. Yet there was no doubt that he was in the way. Everyone told him so. Work would go faster without him. So on Sunday, Mr. Wells drove Bobby out in his car to Uncle Joe's farm and left him there. And the very next Sunday after that, he asked all Bobby's friends — Bill and Jimmy and Ann and Sally and Martha — to go out and visit Bobby at the farm for a whole day.

Seven people are too many to fit into one car, so Mr. Wells took them in his truck instead. Mr. and Mrs. Wells and Martha sat in front, and the rest rode in the back. It was much more fun than riding in a car. Mr. Wells spread an old blanket on the floor for them to sit on. The sides of the truck were low, so they could look out and see everything along the way.

It took an hour to drive to Uncle Joe's farm. First they rode along the highway where the buses run, and then up a real country road past barns and pastures. By and by the road grew narrower and more and more uphill. The truck began to bump. Each time it bumped, the children all shouted, and Mr. Wells called out, "Hold tight, back there!"

At last they came to Uncle Joe's farm. The first person they saw was Bobby. He had blue overalls on, and he looked like a real farmer.

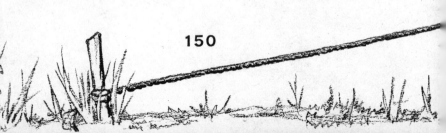

Uncle Joe and Aunt Alice came out to meet them. Uncle Joe said,

"Now run along, all of you. You can play anywhere you like, but don't fall out of the haymow and hurt yourselves, and don't go too near that old billy goat out in the barnyard. He's cross, and he doesn't like strangers."

Of course, the children wanted to see the old billy goat first of all. He was tied by a long rope in the barnyard, and he surely did look cross. He had long, sharp horns and yellow eyes. When the boys got near him, he stood right up on his back legs.

Jimmy said, "Look out! He's getting ready to buck!"

The billy goat was wise. He knew that
he could not get near enough to the boys
to buck them. The rope was long, but
it was not long enough. He shook his
horns and waited.

"I bet if I stayed here long enough,"
Bill said, "I could make that old goat
tame. I'd have him tame enough to pull
a wagon."

He picked a handful of grass and went
nearer, calling, "Here, billy-billy-billy!"

Billy-billy-billy waited. He didn't want
grass. He only wanted someone to come
within reach of those long horns of his.

Bill went a little closer. "See?" he said. "Now you just watch!"

The others were watching. Bill held out his grass. The goat looked at the grass, and he looked at Bill. He stood up on his back legs again. No one saw just what happened. It happened too quickly. But the next minute there was Bill rolling on the ground, and there was the goat, standing quite still and looking round with his yellow eyes, as if to say, "And now, who's next?"

Everyone laughed but Bill. Bill picked himself up, looking very cross.

"If it hadn't been for that rope," Jimmy said, "he'd have bucked you clean through the side of the barn!"

Bill turned on him. "What do you mean, bucked? I just tripped, that's all. Anyone can trip!"

"You tripped good and hard," laughed Jimmy. "Why don't you try again? He's acting real quiet now. Go right up and put your hand on him!"

But Bill had had enough of goats.

"I don't see why anyone wants to keep an old thing like that around," he said. "He's no good for anything except to act mean! I'd rather go to see the horses."

The horses were in the barn. The barn was big, much bigger than the house. It had to be big to hold all Uncle Joe's cows and his horses, and all the hay that they would need to eat through the long winter.

Uncle Joe sold milk. Every morning he carried six big cans of milk in his truck down to the milk station on the highway. He had twenty-four cows, and it took a lot of hay to keep them well fed during the long winter months when they could not go out to pasture.

The hay was in the upstairs part of
the barn. The cows and the horses lived
down below. At one side of the barn
was a big shed where Uncle Joe kept
his truck and his farm tools.

The children stood in the barn doorway.

"Don't you love the smell of a barn!"
said Sally.

The barn did smell nice. It was cool
and dark and clean inside, and it smelled
of hay and of animals. It was an
interesting-looking place, too. All down
one side was a long row of cow stalls.
They were empty now because the cows
were out at pasture. But the horses were
there. They had a place to themselves,
at one end. There were two horses. One
was brown all over, and one was black,
with a white star on his head.

The horses looked very big standing there in their stalls, much bigger than horses look outdoors. But they were gentle animals. When they saw the children, they stretched their heads out and blew softly through their noses. That was their way of saying "Good morning!"

Bobby was not a bit afraid of the horses. He felt that he knew them and that they knew him. He liked the brown horse better because that was the one Uncle Joe always let him ride when the horses went out to get their drink of water every morning.

"I wish we could ride them around the yard," said Jimmy.

He pulled at the brown horse's rope
to make him move around. But the horses
did not want to move. They knew that
it was Sunday, and Sunday was the day
they stayed home in the barn to rest.
They had plenty of moving around all
through the week.

By and by Bill said, "Let's go up in the haymow."

One after another they climbed the ladder to the haymow. The mow was almost empty. It was a good thing that the children had come today for their visit. Very soon Uncle Joe would start cutting the hay in his big meadow. After that the haymow would be full again, much too full to play in. When all the new hay was cut and stored there, it would reach way up to the roof. Now there was just enough hay in the haymow for the children to play in, not too little and not too much.

Walking on the hay was like walking on a great springy feather bed. There was a big pile of it in one corner of the haymow that was fine to slide down. The children slid and jumped and had hay battles till the dust flew up their noses.

They covered up Jimmy in the hay. They covered him until only the tips of his toes showed. Next they covered Ann.

Martha didn't want to be covered up. She was afraid that it would be her turn next. So she slipped away very quietly, down the ladder and out to the barnyard, all by herself.

In one corner of the barnyard was a pen with three baby calves in it. One calf was white with black spots, one was red all over, and one was black with a white face.

Martha loved all baby animals. She didn't always like animals so much after they grew up. But she loved kittens and puppies and baby chickens and baby ducks. Someday, Martha thought, if ever she had a farm of her own, she would have nothing but baby animals on it.

The calves were gentle and friendly, like all Uncle Joe's animals except the cross old billy goat. That was because they had always had good care. Instead of jumping about and acting frightened, the way many baby calves do, they came right up to Martha and poked their noses at her to be petted.

They let Martha touch their noses and their ears. They put out their tongues and licked Martha's hand. Their tongues felt queer, like a cat's tongue.

The little white calf with the black spots was the friendliest of all. By and by he began to get too friendly. He kept pushing closer and closer. He smelled at Martha's shoes, and he smelled at her dress. All at once he put his queer black tongue out and pulled a bit of Martha's skirt into his mouth, just as if it were a bit of hay.

Martha jumped back. But she could not go far. The calf had tight hold of her dress, and he looked as if he did not mean to let go of it, either. Martha pulled, and the calf pulled.

The calf could pull harder than Martha could. Every time he pulled, a little bit more of Martha's skirt disappeared into his mouth.

Martha was frightened. She did not know what to do. In one more minute, she thought, her whole dress would be inside his mouth. And what would happen then? Maybe the calf would keep right on pulling and pull Martha into his mouth, too.

Martha began to yell. She called, "Sally! Sally!" as loudly as she could.

Away up in the haymow Sally heard Martha. She hurried down the ladder and ran into the barnyard. When she saw what was happening, she laughed. She laughed so hard that the calf, too, must have thought it was a great joke. He pulled harder than ever.

Sally pushed him and gave him a little slap on his nose. Still he wouldn't let go. Then Sally just caught hold of him and made him open his mouth.

Martha pulled her dress out.

She looked surprised. She had expected to see her skirt eaten full of holes. But it wasn't. It was all there still, with not one hole in it. But it was very wet where the calf had been rolling it around in his mouth.

"Never mind," said Sally. "Calves like to do that. I guess he thought your dress was good to eat because it has flowers on it! Come on over to the house, and we'll wash it out."

Aunt Alice had plenty of warm water in her kitchen. She washed Martha's dress out and hung it back of the stove.

"There," she said. "That will be dry again in no time. I'd give you one of my dresses, but I guess it would be too big!"

Martha thought so, too. So instead, Aunt Alice tied a kitchen apron round her.

"Now, if you want something to do," Aunt Alice said, "you can finish picking over these berries for me while your dress gets dry."

Martha and Sally sat down on the kitchen doorstep with a big pan between them. By the time the last of the berries were picked over, Martha's dress was all dry and ready to be put on again.

Salting Cattle

After dinner Uncle Joe said, "I'm going to the upper pasture to salt the young cattle. Who wants to come along?"

Everyone wanted to go along, all except Aunt Alice and Mr. and Mrs. Wells. Mr. Wells said right out that he didn't like climbing hills any more. He had climbed plenty of hills when he was a boy. Now, when he came out to spend a day in the country, he'd rather sit still and enjoy himself.

Ann and Martha and Jimmy were very curious. They wanted to know what "salting" meant. They had heard of salting fish and salting meat. But they had never heard of salting cattle, certainly not while the cattle were still running around in the pasture!

Sally and Mr. Wells laughed. Mr. Wells said, "You've heard of putting salt on a bird's tail, haven't you, when you want to catch it? Maybe that is how Uncle Joe catches his cows!"

But the children knew that he was just making fun.

"You'll see when you get there," said Uncle Joe. "Now, Mother, where is the salt?"

Aunt Alice brought the salt box and filled a little bag from it. She tied the bag with string and gave it to Jimmy to carry.

Uncle Joe's land stretched right up the hillside. It was a long walk to the upper pasture where the young cattle grazed — over the meadow first, and along the edge of the corn patch, and then across the brook.

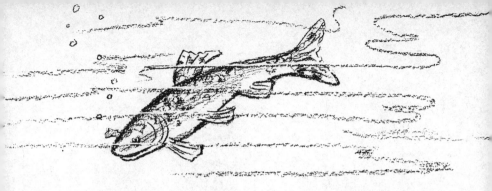

There were steppingstones across the brook, instead of a bridge. Here the brook was not deep, but farther down there was a deep pool. Frogs lived in it, and a fat, lazy old trout. He spent his time right there in the pool, always in the same spot. When the children lay flat on the bank and looked over, deep into the water, they could see nothing at first. Then, by and by, they could make out the trout, like a dark shadow near the bottom. Only his tail was moving, very gently. He didn't want to go either up or down the brook. He was quite happy where he was.

"I could catch him, if I only had a fishing line!" said Jimmy, sounding suddenly like Bill.

Uncle Joe smiled. He said, "You couldn't catch that trout. He's smarter than you think, for all he looks so lazy."

"Did you ever try?" Bill asked.

"No," said Uncle Joe. "Why should I want to catch him? I like him where he is. If I want to go fishing, there are lots of other pools up and down the brook, with fish in them. But that trout is an old friend. He stays quiet there because he knows I won't worry him. If I did, he'd be off like a flash. He's smart. It's because he is smart that he has lived so long."

On the other side of the brook the path began to climb up a hill covered with deep woods. Soon one could not see the sky at all because the trees grew so close together. There was soft moss everywhere, and green ferns. In one place the ferns grew as high as Bobby's head. A little girl could easily get lost in these woods, Martha thought, and never find her way out again. Martha kept close to Sally as they walked.

Ann stopped every minute to gather moss and ferns. She wanted to take them home and make a little garden of them. She carried them in her hat. Each new kind that she saw looked prettier than the last. Soon the hat was quite full. And still Ann kept finding more moss and ferns.

All at once the woods ended. There were grass and rocks and wide blue sky. Uncle Joe led the way up the last little bit of hill, the hardest bit of all to climb, and then he said, "Now turn around and look!"

The children could see the whole countryside spread out below them like a picture. They could see the woods they had just come through, thick and dark. They could see the meadows below, the green corn patch and the brook. There was the home pasture where the cows were grazing. There were Uncle Joe's house and his big red barn, and there, too, was the old billy goat in the barn-yard. Sally could even see very small white squares that must be Aunt Alice's dish towels, hanging on the line by the back door.

Ann said, "Goodness! I never knew we had climbed as high as this!"

"We've been walking uphill for an hour," said Uncle Joe. "Now we'd better have a rest."

All except Uncle Joe were a little out of breath from climbing that last bit of hill. Martha's legs hurt and so did Bobby's, though Bobby would never say so. He was proud of being able to walk so far without help. Last summer Uncle Joe had had to carry him half the way.

"Now, Jimmy," said Uncle Joe, when they had rested, "where is that salt?"

He took the bag from Jimmy and walked over to a big, flat rock near by. He spread the salt out on the rock; and while he was spreading it, he called to the cattle.

Even before he began to call, the cattle had been waiting for him. From every side now they came trotting, big ones and little ones. There were half-grown calves among them, and one old black cow with a crooked horn. They pushed one another with their heads, all crowding round the stone to lick up the salt that Uncle Joe had put out for them. How they loved that salt! It tasted as good to them as candy would have tasted to Ann and Jimmy and Bill.

Long after the last bit of salt had been licked up, the cattle still waited around, hoping for more. But there was no more. Uncle Joe shook out the bag and put it into his pocket. One by one the cattle moved away, back to their grazing. There would be no more salt, they knew, until next Sunday. Only the old black cow still stood there until Uncle Joe gave her a friendly little slap on her nose. Then she, too, turned and walked off.

Uncle Joe said, "Now you know what salting cattle means!"

Bears and Blackberries

Going downhill was much easier than climbing up. It seemed no time at all before they reached the brook once more. Bill looked back at the deep woods through which they had come. The woods looked even thicker, seen from below, than when one was walking through them.

"I bet there are all kinds of wild animals back in those woods," he said.

"There are," replied Uncle Joe.

"Why didn't we see any?" Ann asked.

"Because we made too much noise walking, for one thing," said Uncle Joe. "If you want to see wild things, you have to keep very quiet."

"What kind of things?" Martha wanted to know. She felt glad that she had kept close to Sally and had not gone wandering off by herself.

"Nothing to hurt you," said Uncle Joe, smiling. "There are deer and rabbits back there. But you don't see much of them in summer. The deer keep up in the hills then. But in fall and winter they come down to look for food. Sometimes they come right down around the house."

"Oh, boy!" whispered Jimmy.

And Ann said, "I'd love to see a deer!"

"I can't show you a deer," said Uncle Joe, "but I will show you something else."

They were sitting down to rest on a grassy bank by the side of the brook. Just across from the brook was the home pasture where the big cows grazed; and while Uncle Joe spoke, he was looking straight at it. He said, "See that pile of rocks over there, where I'm pointing? Can you see anything there?"

The children looked. Some of the rocks were yellow and some were gray, but they all looked like rocks. Only Sally laughed because she knew what Uncle Joe meant. She could see what he was looking at, too.

"Now watch," said Uncle Joe.

He put his two fingers in his mouth and blew a sudden, sharp whistle. One of the yellow-colored rocks seemed to drop right into the ground and disappear. Ann and Martha were so surprised that their mouths opened wide.

"That was a woodchuck," said Uncle Joe. "You could not see him before because he looked just the color of the rock he was sitting on. When I whistled, he went into his hole. When woodchucks are feeding, there is always one old fellow on watch. As soon as he thinks there is any danger, he whistles to let the others know. So you can frighten a woodchuck into his hole any time just by whistling at him. There's another one over there."

This time Uncle Joe did not whistle. The children looked where he pointed, and now they could see the woodchuck plainly, sitting up by the mouth of his hole. He looked fat and lazy. But he was not lazy, Uncle Joe said. When he wanted to run, he could run fast enough.

"Woodchucks and rabbits!" said Bill. "I'd like to see something bigger than that. I wish we'd see something real big, like a deer, maybe. Or a bear. Are there ever any bears round here, Uncle Joe?"

"Not right around here," said Uncle Joe. "But there used to be bears once, and not so long ago, either."

"Did you ever see a bear?" Jimmy asked.

"I did," said Uncle Joe, "when I was just about as big as you. And I'll tell you how it happened.

"It was not on this very farm," Uncle Joe began, "so you needn't look so frightened, Martha! It was on another farm across the valley, where we used to live when I was a boy. It was one morning in late summer, just about the time the blackberries were getting ripe, and I was starting out to gather berries with my little sister. There were plenty of blackberries on our land, but the best and sweetest of all grew in a patch the other side of the big pasture, near the brook. That was where we were going that morning.

"I was walking along with my berry pail, thinking how good those blackberries would taste, when I happened to look up. And there, right in the middle of the berry patch, I saw something moving.

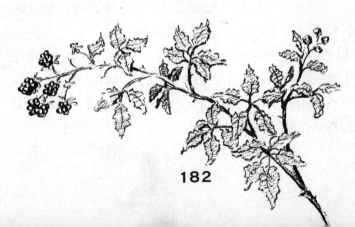

"I couldn't see what it was, but I could see the bushes stirring this way and that, just as if someone was in there picking berries as fast as he could. Now, Mother always counted on those berries to make her blackberry jelly every year, and the first thing I thought was, 'There's someone picking our berries!' And I felt pretty mad.

"I was just going to call out, when all at once I saw a big thing that rose right up on its back legs in the middle of the berry patch and stood there, lifting its nose in the air and waving its arms around and looking for all the world just like some funny old man.

"Well, I'd never seen a bear in my life, but I'd seen pictures of them. There it stood, just about as close to me as that tree there. I didn't need anybody to tell me what it was, either. I just dropped my berry pail and caught my little sister by the hand. We started back for home just as fast as we could run. We ran and ran, and I didn't even stop to look behind me until we were safe in the kitchen. And I said, 'Mother, I just saw a great big bear over in the berry patch!'

"Well, do you know that not one of the family believed me! They thought I was just making it up.

"Mother said, 'Why, Joe, you know there aren't any bears around here! No one ever saw a bear. I guess you just thought you saw it.'

"And my father asked, 'How do you know it was a bear? You never saw a bear in your life.'

"I said, 'I know what a bear looks like, all right, and it looked just like that.'

"My big brother threw his head back and laughed. 'I guess next time you'll be seeing a camel, or a wild bull maybe, right in the middle of the road!'

"Then my aunt called me over. She put her hand on my shoulder, and she said, 'Now, Joe, you know it's wrong to tell lies. You just own right up, and no one will be cross with you. You know you didn't really see a bear!'

"I said, 'I'm sorry, Auntie, but I did see a bear. I truly did.'

"Everyone made fun of me — all but my grandfather. Grandfather had been out when I ran home in the morning, so all he'd heard was what the others told him.

"But next day after breakfast he said to me, 'Come along, Joe. Let's take a walk and find your berry pail, anyway.'

"We walked back over the pasture. I didn't mind going. I wasn't one bit afraid as long as Grandfather was with me. We found the berry pail right where I'd dropped it. We went as far as the berry patch, and there were the bushes all broken down. Someone had been in that berry patch, sure enough.

"Grandfather took me by the hand, and we walked a little farther. We went on down by the brook. We followed the brook a little way, and by and by Grandfather stopped. Right there by the bank was a place where the ground was all soft, and there in the ground were three big footprints! They looked like the prints of a man's bare foot, a man with very long toenails.

"Grandfather said, 'I guess that was your bear, all right, Joe. Here's where he came down to drink. I haven't seen a bear's track in twenty years, but that's what it is.'

"And I guess he was right. It must have been a pretty big bear, too, Grandfather said. He'd come down after our berries; and if I hadn't happened to be walking across lots that morning, no one would ever have seen him at all."

"Did you ever see him again?" Jimmy asked.

"Never," said Uncle Joe. "And what's more, I've never seen hide nor hair of any other bear since. Grandfather said that bear would have been more afraid of us than we were of him. But for a long while after that my sister and I kept away from the blackberry patch; and if we ever did have to go by there, we ran as fast as we could!"

"I bet you were glad you found those footprints," Bill said. "I bet that no one made fun of you any more, either, not after that."

"People made plenty of fun of me," said Uncle Joe. "But you can be sure of one thing. Whatever they poked fun at me about, it wasn't about bears!"

The Padlock

It was fun visiting Uncle Joe's farm. It was fun playing in the haymow and walking up the hill and hearing Uncle Joe's story about the bear. It was fun riding home after dark in Mr. Wells's truck, singing songs all along the way and then tumbling into bed, sleepy and happy, remembering all the nice things that had happened during the day.

But it was not such fun for the Five-and-a-Half Club next morning. For that was the morning they found the padlock on their clubhouse door.

It happened this way.

There had been a lot of things to do lately. There had been baseball every day on the ground back of the schoolhouse, and both Bill and Jimmy liked to play baseball. Ann and Martha had promised to dress dolls for the church fair, and they spent a lot of time over at Ann's house, cutting out and sewing.

Nobody did anything about Mr. Riley's garden. Sally thought that the boys were doing the weeding, and the boys thought that Sally would remember it. But it happened that Sally was busy, too.

And, in the meantime, the weeds were growing up thick and fast.

On Sunday, while the Five-and-a-Half's were all having such a good time at Uncle Joe's farm, Mr. Riley went out to look at his garden. He had never seen so many weeds in his garden before. And no one else ever had, either.

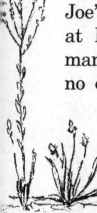

Mr. Riley was pretty cross.

He had told those young ones just what he would do if they did not keep their promise about weeding. And now he was going to do it. He took a strong padlock, fastened it on the shed door, and snapped it tight.

"That will teach them!" said Mr. Riley.

Mr. Riley was cross, but he was not nearly so angry as Bill and Jimmy were when they went over early on Monday morning and saw what had happened to the clubhouse.

"Mean old thing," said Bill, giving the door a kick. "I was going to work in that garden today after we get through playing. But I wouldn't touch it now, not if it got knee-high with weeds! And I just hope it does. I hope it doesn't rain all summer and everything he has in it dries up! I hope — "

"Where's Bunson?" cried Jimmy suddenly. "What do you suppose he did with Bunson?"

The two boys looked at each other.

"Bunson will die, locked up in there," said Bill. "How does old Mr. Riley think we're going to feed him?"

They listened at the door. Always before, they could hear Mr. Bunson moving around in his pen. But today there was not a sound.

Maybe Bunson had died already. Jimmy looked ready to cry. They had left Bunson alone all yesterday, but Mrs. Green had promised to give him something to eat. Suppose Mrs. Green had forgotten?

Jimmy was wondering just how long a rabbit could live without food.

"If he's done anything to Bunson — " Bill began in an angry voice.

"He couldn't be as mean as that!" Jimmy cried.

"He could," said Bill. "A person who's mean enough to put on that padlock would be mean enough to do anything!"

But there Bill was wrong. Mr. Riley was just. He had no fault to find with Mr. Bunson. It wasn't Mr. Bunson's fault that the garden was not weeded. If Bunson had been running around out-doors, instead of being shut up in a pen, he would have cleaned up that garden in his own way, weeds and all.

Before locking the door, Mr. Riley had picked Bunson up, pen and all, and had carried him over to Mrs. Green's back doorstep. It was hard work, too. The rabbit was heavy. So was the pen. And Mr. Riley was none too strong in his back. But it's surprising how strong a person can be when he is really cross!

When the boys ran over to Sally's
house, there was Bunson all safe and
sound by Sally's back steps. Sally was
giving him some carrot tops.

Sally was not feeling any too cheerful,
either. It is not pleasant, when you have
worked and worked over anything the
way they all had done over that clubhouse,
to have it suddenly taken away from you.
No one could possibly like it. But Sally
had heard the bad news the evening
before when she first reached home, so
she had had all night to think about it.
By now she was feeling a little better,
but she was still cross, not so much at
Mr. Riley as at the boys.

"If you'd kept that garden weeded the
way I told you," she said to Bill and
Jimmy, "this would never have happened."

But the boys felt that if it was their job to weed the garden, it was Sally's job to remind them. They sat on the back steps, each of them feeling very ill-used, and watched Bunson enjoying his carrot tops. At least Bunson was safe, and that was something.

"I'd just like to get even with that old man," said Bill by and by. "I'll do it, too."

"How long do you suppose he'll keep that padlock on there?" Jimmy wondered.

"For just as long as you have let his garden go without weeding, if he has good sense," said Mrs. Green, who had just come out to hang up her dish towels. "That weeding job was your way of paying rent. If people don't pay their rent, they can't expect to keep their houses."

The three looked at her in surprise. They never expected Mrs. Green to say a thing like that. Up to now she had always been ready to take their side. If Mrs. Green was going to turn against them, too, things must be at a pretty pass.

Mrs. Green went on hanging up her dish towels, just as if she did not know, quite well, what was in their minds.

"I guess you're right about it," Jimmy said after a while. "It's all our own fault."

"I've been thinking, Mrs. Green," Bill said, "that maybe if you were to go and speak to Mr. Riley, it would be a good idea. I mean, it isn't any good our speaking to him because he's angry at us. But maybe if you went there and asked him, nicely — "

"Asked him what?" said Mrs. Green. "I have nothing to ask Mr. Riley. If you want to do any asking, you'll have to do it yourselves. And besides," she added, "I don't think today is a good time to ask him anything. Not with that garden looking the way it does!"

It seemed that there was no help to be had from Mrs. Green. If things were ever to be put right, it would have to be done some other way.

But it is not always easy to set things right, once they have gone wrong.

The boys did not feel like weeding Mr. Riley's garden as long as Mr. Riley kept that padlock on the door.

Mr. Riley did not feel like taking that padlock off until his garden was weeded.

So that was how it was.

At home the boys and girls were careful to say nothing about what had happened. But news has a way of getting round. One evening at supper Mrs. Baker asked, "Why don't you use your playhouse any more? Have you got tired of it?"

And then, of course, Jimmy had to tell her. Mrs. Baker said, "So he put a padlock on it, did he?" And Mr. Baker said, "Well, well!"

That was all. But Jimmy and Bill and Ann and Martha all knew just how their fathers and mothers felt about the matter. Strangely enough, they seemed to feel just the same as Mrs. Green did.

So the days went on, and the only one who was at all happy was Mr. Bunson. Bunson liked living on the Greens' back doorstep. He could look out from his pen and see everything that went on. Mrs. Green talked to him through her kitchen window. She fed him apple skins and bits of bread.

He didn't care if that padlock stayed on the shed door for ever and ever!

You Can't Tame a Jack Rabbit

In the meantime, out on the farm, Uncle Joe had started to cut his big hay meadow. First he cut down some of the long grass near the gate, just enough to let his horses get by. Then he took the mower in and began to drive it round and round the meadow.

Bobby liked to watch the mower at work and to hear the sound it made. When the hay was all cut and had dried in the sun, he would help to rake it into piles. Then he would be able to ride on the hay wagon.

It took two days to cut the big hay meadow. Uncle Joe had two boys to help him with the haymaking. They came early in the morning and stayed all day.

While Bobby was watching the mower
at work, one of the boys came over to
him. He was carrying something carefully
inside his hat. He said to Bobby, "Guess
what I have for you."

Bobby guessed that it was a turtle.
They often found turtles in the meadow.
He looked inside the hat. But it wasn't
a turtle. It was a baby jack rabbit. The
boys had found it in the long grass where
they were cutting hay.

Bobby was all excited. For a long while he had wanted a pet rabbit of his very own.

Baby jack rabbits do not look just like other baby rabbits. They have longer back legs and bigger, longer ears. This one looked all legs and ears and eyes when Bobby first saw it inside the boy's hat. It was small, and it was frightened.

"You can keep it," said the farmer boy. "If you put it in a box, it won't get out. It's too young to jump far."

The boy put the baby rabbit into Bobby's hands. The rabbit lay quite still, and Bobby could feel its heart going bump-bump under the soft coat.

"That's because it's afraid," the boy said.

Uncle Joe said, "Jack rabbits are not like other rabbits, Bobby. You can't tame jack rabbits. They are too wild."

But Bobby was sure that he could tame this one. The baby rabbit did not seem a bit wild.

Bobby ran to the house. He wanted to ask Aunt Alice for a box to keep his rabbit in. But Aunt Alice had a better idea. There was a little empty room upstairs where she kept apples in winter. There were no apples there now. Aunt Alice said that Bobby could keep his rabbit in this room. That would be better than a box because the rabbit could run about and stretch its long legs.

"What will it eat?" Bobby asked.

"Grass and leaves," said Aunt Alice. "When they have finished cutting the hay meadow, you can let it go again. Then it will find food for itself."

"But I don't want to let it go," Bobby said. "I'm going to tame it and take it back home with me."

When Bobby put the rabbit down on the floor, it just sat there for a minute, quite still. Then it hopped over to one corner very slowly and sat there, looking at the wall.

Bobby brought some grass and put it down in front of the baby rabbit's nose.

But the rabbit did not want to eat. It would not look at the grass, and it would not look at Bobby. It just looked at the wall.

"Maybe the rabbit wants a drink," said Bobby. "It's hot in the hay meadow."

So he brought some water in a bowl. But the rabbit did not want water, either. It didn't want anything Bobby could give.

Bobby thought, "Maybe it doesn't like to be watched. Maybe it will eat better if I'm not here."

He closed the door and ran back to the hay meadow.

Every little while during the day Bobby ran upstairs to see how his jack rabbit was getting along. Each time the rabbit was sitting there in its corner. It had not moved once. It had not eaten its food, and it had not touched the water. It just sat there.

Next day Uncle Joe asked, "How is your rabbit getting along?"

"It's quite tame," Bobby answered, "but it won't eat anything yet."

"Let's go see it," said Uncle Joe.

They went up to the little room. Sunlight came through the window. The little rabbit was still sitting in its corner, watching the wall.

"See how tame it is already," Bobby cried. "It doesn't mind my petting one bit."

But the little rabbit was not really tame. It was just very, very frightened. It was too frightened to move, even when Bobby touched it.

"Does it sit there all the time?" asked Uncle Joe.

"It likes that corner," said Bobby. "That's its house. It can run around any time it wants to. But it likes to sit there."

"Hum," said Uncle Joe. He looked at the grass on the floor.

"I guess the rabbit just isn't hungry," said Bobby.

"I guess it isn't," said Uncle Joe. But he didn't say anything more.

All that day, and the next day, everyone was busy in the hay meadow. All the grass had been cut and left to dry into hay. Now the hay must be raked into piles and carried home on the hay wagon. Everyone helped. Even Aunt Alice put on her big shady hat and came out to rake, too.

In between the hay rides Bobby went to see his rabbit. Each time he found it sitting there in the corner. Bobby brought it hay and grass. He brought it everything he could think of. He brought bread and milk and carrots. But the little jack rabbit would not eat any of them.

No one asked Bobby about his rabbit. Bobby was glad. He still felt sure that he could tame that rabbit, but he did not want to talk about it.

The very last load of hay had been raked up and carried home. The meadow was empty. But the haymow in the barn was full. It was full nearly to the top. Now the cows and horses would have plenty to eat all winter.

Uncle Joe said, "We've had good weather for our haymaking."

"Indeed we have," said Aunt Alice.

"And Bobby has worked like a real farmer, too," said Uncle Joe.

They were at the supper table. Uncle Joe smiled at Bobby. But Bobby did not smile back. He was looking at his plate.

There were tears in Bobby's eyes. He did not want anyone to see them. He was afraid that if he did not keep very still, one of those tears would roll right down onto his plate.

Bobby did not eat much supper. After the dishes were cleared away, Uncle Joe said, "Come on, Bobby. You and I have been working hard all day. Suppose we take a little ride."

Uncle Joe got his car from the barn, and they drove off.

It was beginning to get dark. Uncle Joe drove slowly. He did not talk much — just looked about him. Bobby did not want to talk, either.

They turned into a narrow road. Long grass and weeds grew on either side of the way.

By and by Uncle Joe stopped the car for a minute. He felt in his pocket for his pipe and matches. Bobby was looking straight ahead, down the road.

All at once Bobby cried out, "Look! There's a rabbit!"

"Lots of rabbits round here," said Uncle Joe. "I often come up here and watch them."

Uncle Joe turned the car lights off. There was the rabbit right in the middle of the road. It was a baby rabbit. Soon a second baby rabbit came out from the long grass. The two rabbits began to play together. Then another little rabbit joined them. And then another. Before long Bobby could count five of them, all playing along the road and in and out of the weeds.

"Maybe they are brothers and sisters," Bobby said.

"I wouldn't wonder," said Uncle Joe. "Lots of rabbit families live round here. There are baby rabbits all around in these meadows. Isn't that one pretty, sitting up there?"

"I guess they have fun," said Bobby.

"I guess they do," said Uncle Joe.

They watched the rabbits a while longer. Then Uncle Joe turned his car around, and they drove back home.

Bobby was quiet all the way. He was thinking about those baby rabbits. When they were putting the car away, he said in a small voice, "Uncle Joe —"

"Yes?"

"Uncle Joe," said Bobby. He stopped, and then began again. "I was thinking. I was thinking that maybe — maybe I'll let my rabbit go."

Uncle Joe looked very much surprised. He said, "But I thought you wanted to tame it, for a pet?"

"I did want to," said Bobby. "But I guess I don't want to tame it any more. I'd rather let it go."

Uncle Joe waited. Bobby said, "I want to let it go right now — tonight!"

"Fine," said Uncle Joe. "It's your rabbit. You do just as you like."

Bobby ran to the house. He got his flashlight and opened the door of the little upstairs room. The jack rabbit was still sitting in its corner. Its eyes looked big and round with the flashlight shining on them. Around on the floor lay all the food it had not eaten. Bobby picked the rabbit up. It felt very small and light under its fur.

Bobby ran downstairs in a great hurry to where Uncle Joe was waiting for him, and they walked out together to the big hay meadow.

The moon was coming up. It gave just enough light to see by. When they had walked a little way out into the meadow, Bobby asked, "Do you think this would be a good place?"

"I think it would be a fine place," said Uncle Joe.

Bobby set the little jack rabbit down on the ground. For a moment the baby rabbit just sat there. It could not believe that it was really free. Then it gave itself a shake. It shook its feet, and it shook its ears. It took a great big hop into the air, and off it went, hopping down the meadow, faster and faster, as if it would never stop.

"Do you suppose it has a lot of brothers and sisters over there?" Bobby asked when the little rabbit had hopped right out of sight.

"I'm pretty sure it has," said Uncle Joe. "It was running as if it knew right where to find them, too."

As they walked back to the house, Bobby held Uncle Joe's hand very tight.

"I'm glad I let it go," Bobby said.

Two weeks later Uncle Joe drove into town. When he came back, he brought a square box with holes in it. Bobby untied the string and opened the box.

Inside there was a baby rabbit, brown and white. Except for his brown spots, he looked just like Mr. Bunson.

"That," said Uncle Joe, "is the kind of rabbit you can really tame!"

Changes

Mrs. Riley missed the children. With
Mr. Riley away at work all day she was
sometimes lonesome. The children were
company for her. She liked to watch
them from her kitchen window.

To begin with, they had painted the
old shed, and that made a great change.
Instead of being ugly, it was now nice
to look at. She had watched the boys
and girls at their painting, day by day,
and she had taken a great interest in
seeing them carry their things over and
fix the place up. She liked to watch
what they were doing and to wonder
what they were going to do next.

Then there had been the party. Mrs. Riley had liked that, too.

Now everything was changed. The shed was locked. The garden seemed lonely. The boys and girls stayed at home or played over in Mrs. Green's garden. Mrs. Riley could hear their voices, but she could not see them. It was not like old times. She wished that something could be done about it.

There was no use speaking to Mr. Riley about it. Mrs. Riley had lived with Mr. Riley long enough to know that when once Mr. Riley made up his mind, no amount of talking in the world would make him change it. That was the way he was.

Mr. Riley was not happy, either. His leg had started worrying him again just as soon as he started weeding. Mr. Riley really needed help with that garden, and he knew it. It was so long since he had done any bending over that now it tired him more than ever. His leg hurt, and his back hurt, too.

For many weeks Mr. Riley had been having an easy time. When he came home of an evening, all he had to do was to walk out and look at his garden. Maybe he would gather some beans or pick off a worm or two here and there. But he did not have to bend over and pull up weeds.

Now he had to work, and work hard. He had to reach down and pull up those weeds one by one.

Every evening he had to bend his tired old back, over and over again.

Every evening Mrs. Riley had to sit by her kitchen window and watch him doing it.

Mr. Riley began to wish, very much, that he had never put that padlock on at all. But it was too late now. He did not see what he could do about it without going back on his word. And Mr. Riley never went back on his word.

The Thunderstorm

Every summer the Sunday school had a picnic. All the teachers who had cars, and the mothers who had cars, met and drove the children out to the place where the picnic was to be. They started early in the morning and spent the whole day.

Every year they went to a different place. One year they had gone to the seashore, and one year they had gone to the woods. This year they were going to the river.

Everyone had been looking forward to the picnic and talking about it. Bill and Jimmy had their fishing lines all ready. They would be able to fish in the river, and there would be boats, too. Ann said that she wanted to catch lobsters.

"You don't get lobsters in a river," said Bill. "Lobsters live in the sea."

"You do, too!" said Ann. "Once we went to a little brook, and I turned some stones over, and there was a tiny baby lobster under them."

"That wasn't a real lobster," Jimmy told her. "Real lobsters are big. That thing you found just looked like a lobster, but it wasn't really."

But Ann wouldn't give in. "Anyway," she said, "that's what I want to catch. I don't like to fish with a fishing line. I like things I can catch with my hands."

"You'd better catch tadpoles, then," said Bill.

"I will," said Ann. "You catch your old fish, and Martha and I will catch tadpoles. We'll bring them home in a jar, and then we can watch them turn into frogs. That's more fun than fishing!"

Ann had made a little garden with the ferns and moss she brought back from Uncle Joe's farm. She and Martha had set them all out in a wooden box. On the bottom of the box they had put a bowl of water with earth all round it, and that was their pond. It would be nice to have tadpoles in that pond. Then, when they turned into frogs, they could hop about among the ferns and moss.

Martha thought that it would be a lovely idea, too. But on the day of the picnic, Martha could not go.

It was a funny thing about Martha. Nearly always, when she heard about something exciting that was going to happen, she got sick. She did not get sick after the excitement was over, which would not have mattered so much. She got sick before.

She was sick the night before the picnic. Her mother said that she could not go. Mrs. Strong did not want Martha running about in the hot sun all day and maybe sitting on wet grass. Martha would have to stay at home. She could look at books and cut out paper dolls in bed; and at dinnertime, if she felt better, she could get up. It was too bad to miss the picnic, but Martha could have another picnic some other day and ask all her friends.

Martha spent the whole morning in bed. And sure enough, by dinnertime, she did feel better. She was well enough to get up and play out on the porch.

In the afternoon Martha's mother had to go downtown. "I'll be home just as soon as I can," she said to Martha. "I have locked the back door and closed the windows, and you can stay right here on the porch. If a storm comes up, you can run over to Mrs. Baker's house and stay with her until I get back."

Martha did not mind being left alone. It was fun. It made her feel grown-up to keep house all by herself.

She sat on the porch in the big rocking chair and rocked. It was very quiet all around. Nearly everyone was away at the picnic. Mrs. Wells had gone with her car to drive the children. Mrs. Green was away, too. She had not gone to the picnic, but she had gone downtown. Martha had seen her waiting at the corner for the bus. Mrs. Baker was at home, and so was Mrs. Riley. Today Mrs. Riley had been washing clothes. Martha could see a whole row of clean washing, hanging out on the line by Mrs. Riley's back door.

Martha sat and watched the cars go by on the road. She amused herself by guessing how many cars would go by before she could count up to one hundred. If she guessed right, she won. When she got near the end, she would count very slowly, hoping that just one more car would come by so that she could win. She was so busy counting that she never noticed that the sun had gone in and big dark clouds were rolling up.

All at once the telephone bell gave a queer little tinkle. Martha jumped. She knew right away what that meant. It meant that a storm was coming up. Always, before a storm, the telephone bell would make that funny little noise.

Martha looked round her. The leaves on the trees were hanging straight and still. The sky had become very black. She heard the first sound of thunder. Then the rain began to fall in big, splashy drops.

Martha did not like storms. They always frightened her. If there was a storm coming, she did not want to be all alone in the house.

If she ran fast, she could still get to Mrs. Baker's house before it stormed hard. Martha started to go down the steps. But right on the top step she stood still and stared.

She was looking at Mrs. Riley's house, over the way. Mrs. Riley had not taken her washing in. That was what Martha was looking at.

Always, when it started to rain, Mrs. Riley took her washing in. She was the very last person in the world to leave her washing out there on the line to get all wet and splashed.

But there they still hung, all those clean, white clothes. They were getting wet through. The rain was coming down faster and faster. Why didn't Mrs. Riley come out and take them in?

Martha waited. She wondered whether anything queer could have happened over at Mrs. Riley's house. All at once there came a flash and a big roll of thunder.

And then Jip began to bark.

Jip belonged to Mr. and Mrs. Riley. He was a big dog, black all over. He was not a bad dog. But he was old and cross. Mr. Riley kept him tied on the back porch.

Jip was barking now, Martha knew, because there was a storm coming, and Jip did not like storms. He was afraid of them, just as Martha was. When there was a storm coming, Mrs. Riley always took Jip into the house. He wanted to be taken into the house now.

Why didn't Mrs. Riley let Jip into the house? And why didn't Mrs. Riley take her clean washing in?

Martha felt sure now that there must be something very wrong over at Mrs. Riley's house.

Martha hated thunder. And she hated those great blue flashes. At this very minute she wanted, more than anything else, to run over to Mrs. Baker's house and into Mrs. Baker's kitchen. There she would be safe and comfortable with the doors closed and all the lights on.

All along the road hung wires, telephone wires and wires that carried the light for all the houses. When it stormed, flashes of light sometimes ran up and down along them. Martha would have to cross the road right under those wires to get to Mrs. Riley's house. Suppose a big flash came just when she was under those wires?

Martha did not want to think about that, but she could not help it. She took a big breath. Then she ran down the steps and right across the road over to Mrs. Riley's house.

What Happened to Mrs. Riley

Mrs. Riley was glad that she had got her washing done so early. Now it would be all nice and dry by afternoon. She sat down and rested and ate her dinner. Then she thought that, as it was such a nice day, she would do something else.

Down in the cellar there was a shelf full of glass jars. Every summer Mrs. Riley put canned fruit in them. Soon it would be time to can fruit again. Mrs. Riley thought that it would be a very good idea to get all those jars up today and wash them so that they would be clean and ready.

She opened the cellar door and started to go down. But on the top step she slipped and fell all the way to the bottom. When she tried to get up, she found that she could not move. Her leg was badly hurt.

There was nothing to do. It was no use calling for help. Mrs. Riley might call as loudly as she liked. No one would hear her but Jip, and Jip was no help. Mrs. Wells was out, and Mrs. Green was out, and all the other houses were too far away for anyone to hear.

All that Mrs. Riley could do was to sit there on the cellar floor and wait until Mr. Riley came home from his work.

It seemed a long, long time.

Two Is Company

At most times Martha would have been afraid of Jip. But today she was too frightened at the storm to be afraid of anything else. She ran right past Jip as if he had not been there.

Martha banged on the back door. No one answered. Jip barked again and wagged his tail. Martha opened the door and went in.

There was no one in the kitchen. There was no one in the front room. And then Martha heard Mrs. Riley's voice. It seemed to come from way down under the floor.

Martha saw the cellar door standing open. She looked down. There at the bottom of the cellar steps sat Mrs. Riley.

"Thank goodness!" Mrs. Riley said.

She was glad that someone had come at last. She looked up at Martha, and Martha looked down at her, very much surprised.

"I thought I would have to sit here all day," Mrs. Riley said. "Can you get down those steps, child? Be careful you don't slip!"

Martha ran down. "What happened?" she asked. "Did you hurt yourself?"

"I hurt my leg," said Mrs. Riley. "It hurts every time I try to move. But maybe, if you give me a hand, I could get up."

Martha tried hard. She took hold of both Mrs. Riley's hands and pulled. But it was of no use. Mrs. Riley was a heavy woman. It would take someone much bigger and stronger than Martha to pull Mrs. Riley up. And even if Martha could help Mrs. Riley to her feet, she could never get her back up those cellar steps.

The more Mrs. Riley tried to move, the more her leg hurt.

"It's no use," she said at last. "I guess I will just have to go on sitting here until Mr. Riley gets home."

"I could bring someone," said Martha. There was no telephone in Mrs. Riley's house. The nearest place where Martha could get help would be Mrs. Baker's.

"I won't have you running out again in this storm," said Mrs. Riley. "We must wait until it is over. I've sat here a good while, and I guess I can sit a while longer, now I've got someone to keep me company. But there is one thing you can do, if you like. You can go and unfasten Jip's collar, if you aren't afraid, and let him in the house."

Jip stood quite still while Martha unfastened his collar. Then he ran right into the kitchen and hid himself in a dark corner under the table. That was the place he always liked to be in, in a thunderstorm.

It seemed as if that storm would never stop. It banged and it flashed, and the rain came down in rivers.

But for the first time in her life Martha did not mind it. She was thinking too much about Mrs. Riley to worry about the storm. The cellar was safe and dry. It was not likely that they would be hit, down there.

"I guess a cellar is a good place to be in, in a storm," said Martha.

"It is," said Mrs. Riley.

Then she told Martha about the time when she was a little girl and lived on a farm out West. There were bad windstorms there; and whenever a big wind came up, everyone had to go down in the cellar and shut the door tight and stay there until the wind was over.

Mrs. Riley kept on talking. She thought that it would keep her from thinking about her leg. Martha liked to listen. All through the storm they sat there in the cellar.

At last the storm was nearly over. It was still raining hard, but Martha did not mind rain. She ran over to Mrs. Baker's house to tell her about Mrs. Riley.

And then things began to happen fast. Mrs. Baker called up Mr. Riley at the railroad yard, and she called up the neighbors down the road. They came over to the Riley house, and among them they helped Mrs. Riley up the cellar steps and into her bedroom.

Mrs. Riley was very glad. She had been sitting in that cellar quite long enough. "Though what I would have done without Martha," she said, "I can't think!"

In the middle of it all Martha's mother came back. She had waited downtown until the storm was over. She was surprised to find Martha over at Mrs. Riley's house and to hear what had happened while she was away.

As for Martha, for days and days she could never see a line of washing without thinking of Mrs. Riley and the cellar steps.

How It Was All Settled

Ann caught three tadpoles at the picnic. Two were just plain tadpoles. The other one had two little back legs, just beginning to grow. Before long it would turn into a real frog.

Ann and Martha put the tadpoles into the pond in their garden. There was just room enough for them to move around.

One day Ann said, "I think it would be nice if we took our garden over to Mrs. Riley's house. Mrs. Riley can't get out to see her own garden now. If we take her ours, she can keep it right in her room to look at."

Everyone was doing things for Mrs. Riley these days. Mrs. Green and Sally went over every day to do her housework. Ann's mother and Martha's mother took turns cooking her dinner while Mr. Riley was away at work. Ann and Martha were in and out all the time.

Mrs. Riley liked to have them come over. Sitting there all day long, with her leg up on a chair, was tiresome, and it was nice to have company. She had never before had so much company as she had now.

The boys came to visit, too. At first they only poked their heads round the door to ask how Mrs. Riley was. Then one day they heard Mrs. Riley telling Ann and Martha and Sally more stories about the time when she was a little girl and lived out West. The boys sat down on the floor to listen, too.

It is funny, the boys and girls thought, how things sometimes turn out. If Mrs. Riley had not fallen down those steps and hurt her leg, they might never have found out what a nice person she really was. They wondered whether, if Mr. Riley fell downstairs, he would turn into a nice person, too. But it did not seem likely. Things do not work the same way with everyone. Maybe it would make Mr. Riley worse instead of better. You never can tell.

Meantime, Mr. Riley stayed just about the way he always had been. And every evening when they heard his step coming up the front walk, the children always slipped out by the back door.

One morning, after they had been visiting at Mrs. Riley's house, Bill said to Jimmy, "I wish there was something we could do for Mrs. Riley. The girls are all helping over there, and all we do is just sit around."

"That's right," Jimmy said. "The girls do so much that there's nothing left for us. I wish Mrs. Riley would want her house painted, or something like that."

He looked back at Mrs. Riley's house. It certainly didn't need painting. Mrs. Riley's fence did not need painting, either. Everything about the Riley place was very well cared for — all but the garden. For days and days Mr. Riley had not had one minute to work in his garden. It was a sight.

The boys looked at each other. They
were both thinking the same thing.

Then Jimmy said, "That garden is going
to be all spoiled unless someone gets to
work on it."

"Just look at those weeds," said Bill.
"Nothing else has room to grow. Pretty
soon there won't be a bean or a carrot
fit to eat! You'd think Mr. Riley might
do something about it."

"I guess he's too busy taking care of Mrs. Riley," Jimmy said.

"I guess he must be," said Bill.

That night Jimmy lay awake. He was thinking how nice that garden used to look when he and Bill took care of it. It seemed too bad to have it all spoiled now. And all because of a padlock!

Early next morning Jimmy took his rake and went over on tiptoe into the Riley garden. He didn't want anyone to see him.

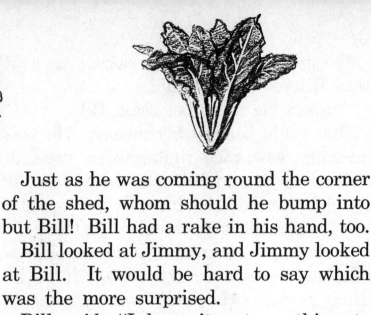

Just as he was coming round the corner
of the shed, whom should he bump into
but Bill! Bill had a rake in his hand, too.

Bill looked at Jimmy, and Jimmy looked
at Bill. It would be hard to say which
was the more surprised.

Bill said, "I haven't got anything to
do this morning, so I might as well pull
a few of those weeds out. It makes me
sick to see a garden looking that way."

"Me too," Jimmy said. "I was thinking
just the same thing, myself."

242

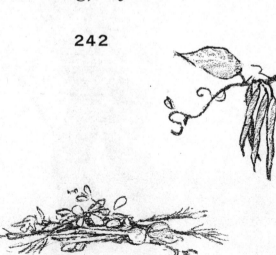

"Guess we'd better get to work, then," Bill growled. "But I tell you one thing," he added. "If I weed this garden, I'm doing it for Mrs. Riley, not for Mr. Riley. And don't you make any mistake about it, either!"

When Bill worked, he worked hard. He pulled those weeds up now as if he were fighting a battle. All morning the boys weeded and raked; and by the time they had finished, the garden looked very different.

243

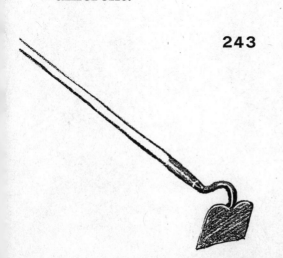

"I guess that will give Mr. Riley a surprise when he gets home," Jimmy said.
"I guess it will," said Bill.

But if Mr. Riley noticed the garden, he never said one word. The padlock stayed right where it was.

Then one evening Mr. Riley came home early. He set his lunch box down on the table. He took off his coat and hung it over a chair. Then he said, "I want to talk to those young ones."

He called the boys and girls in. They felt uneasy because they did not know what Mr. Riley was going to say. But Mr. Riley knew, all right. He had been thinking it over for a whole week. He still felt that the boys had acted bad about his garden. But if there was one thing that Mr. Riley loved better than his garden, it was Mrs. Riley. And he could not help thinking how Mrs. Riley might have stayed there alone for hours and hours, at the bottom of those cellar steps, if it had not been for Martha.

For days Mr. Riley had been wondering just what he could do about that padlock. And now he knew.

"I want to talk to you about that playhouse," he began. "Now, when we started out, we made a bargain. I was to let you use the shed, and you were to keep my garden weeded. A bargain is a bargain, and bargains are made to be kept."

Mr. Riley waited a minute. The children did not say one word. Mrs. Riley did not say a word. She sat there in the big armchair and went on with her sewing.

"I've got eyes as good as most," Mr. Riley went on. "I've seen how Ann and Martha and Sally come over here every day, washing dishes and cleaning house, when they might be out playing. I've seen how you boys have been pulling up weeds when you thought I wasn't looking. And I don't forget how Martha came all the way over here in the storm because she thought Mrs. Riley was in trouble. I like Martha. I think Martha is a brave little girl.

"All the same," Mr. Riley said, "I don't go back on my word. I've never done it yet, and I'm not going to do it now. Our bargain didn't work, and I'm not going to have any more of it. From now on, I'm not going to rent that playhouse to anybody. What do you think, Mother?"

Mrs. Riley looked up from her sewing. She said, "I think you are quite right."

The boys and girls were disappointed.
Maybe they had made a mistake about
Mrs. Riley, after all. And just when
they had been hoping that maybe everything would turn out all right!

"But there is one thing I can do," Mr.
Riley went on. "I can do this."

He took a piece of paper and a pen
and sat down at the kitchen table to
write. He wrote slowly and with great
care. When he had finished, he gave the
paper to Martha. She read it out loud.

It said,

> I hereby give the shed in my back garden to
>
>   Martha Strong
>
> to use as she thinks fit.
>
>   T. Andrew Riley

Martha stared. She couldn't believe her eyes. She said, "Does that mean it's really and truly mine?"

"It means you can do just what you like with it," said Mr. Riley, and his eyes twinkled.

"Then I can give it back to our club," said Martha.

"You can pull it down if you want to," said Mr. Riley. "I have nothing to do with it any more."

The boys and girls felt like shouting. They all cried out at once, "Thank you, Mr. Riley! Thank you ever so much!"

"Don't thank me," said Mr. Riley. "If you want to thank anyone, you can thank Martha. If it wasn't for Martha, you wouldn't have that playhouse at all."

"And if it wasn't for Martha's being sick, she wouldn't have stayed home from the picnic," said Ann, "and she wouldn't have noticed Mrs. Riley's washing."

"And if it wasn't for the storm, she'd never have thought there was anything wrong," said Jimmy.

"And if I'd had sense and looked where I was going," added Mrs. Riley, "I would never have fallen down those cellar steps in the first place!"

Everyone laughed, and Sally said, "It's just like the House that Jack Built!"

Bill and Jimmy put in, "We'll weed your garden every single day, Mr. Riley. You see if we don't!"

"That," said Mr. Riley, "will be just as you feel about it. If I were you, I wouldn't make too many promises. You might change your minds." But he smiled as he said it. Funny how that smile changed Mr. Riley's whole face!

"And now," Mr. Riley added, "I'd better go and take that padlock off before I change my mind!"

But the children were not afraid of that. Mr. Riley never changed his mind. He had said so.

Sally stayed behind with Mrs. Riley. From the window they could see Mr. Riley going across the garden, with Bill and Ann and Jimmy and Martha all crowding at his heels. They were going to watch him take the padlock off.

Sally said, "I think Mr. Riley is right, too. He is wiser than anyone I know. If you do things because you are friends with people and want to help them, it's much better than doing them just because you have to. One way you are doing something you like, and the other you are doing something you don't like."

Mrs. Riley only smiled. She, too, was wise. And she had found all that out for herself, long ago.

Word List

This book is a *Parallel Third Reader* to follow the Basic Third Reader, *If I Were Going*. Its purpose is (1) to use in new and interesting stories the basic vocabulary of the *Pre-Primers, Primer,* and *First, Second,* and *Third Readers* of THE ALICE AND JERRY BOOKS; (2) to keep the introduction of new words to a minimum—in this book 8.36% of the accumulated basic vocabulary; (3) to develop confidence, power, and pleasure in reading by supplying content well within the range of a pupil's ability.

Only 114 new words are introduced in the book. Three pages introduce three new words each, eighteen pages two new words each, and sixty-nine pages one new word each. On one hundred sixty pages, no new words are introduced.

5 school	64–65	119 breathing	185
vacation	66 tub	thumping	186 auntie
6 Sally	67–68	120–121	truly
7–9	69 sorted	122 mad	187 (foot)prints
10 twinkly	70 crazy	123	188
11	71 sh-h	124 rubbed	189 pad(lock)
12 club	twitched	125 locked	190–192
13–16	72–73	126 stairs	193 none
17 bargain	74 tame	127 hose	194 carrot
18 Riley	75 poked	128–129	possibly
shed	finger	130 leaped	195 ill(-used)
19–20	cloth	burned	196 speak
21 beans	76–77	131–132	197–198
22	78 hunt	133 wasp	199 mower
23 costs	person	smarter	200–205
24 growled	79–80	134 stung	206 plate
25–27	81 spent	whose	207 cleared
28 broom	82 write	135–142	208–209
29 (wall)paper	83 buttons	143 hit	210 fur
30–33	84	144–147	211 moment
34 past	85 odd(-shaped)	148 aunt	free
35–37	86 sewing	149–150	212
38 measure	87 sleeves	151 haymow	213 ugly
39–42	88	buck	214 amount
43 (paint)brush	89 lying	152–153	bending
44–46	90–93	154 rather	215
47 packages	94 main	155–157	216 thunder(storm)
48–49	95 women	158 feather	217 tiny
50 measles	96 department	dust	218 sick
51 towel	97–103	159	219 porch
52–55	104 thread	160 tongues	220–221
56 streak	105–106	licked	222 telephone
57	107 chocolate	pushing	stared
58 quite	108	161–164	223–224
59 plants	109 parcel	165 salting	225 wires
60	110	166	226–234
61 paste	111 plan	167 trout	235 neighbors
62 job	pole	168–169	236–239
patted	112	170 ferns	240 unless
63 dipped	113 bet	171–179	241–244
lots	114–118	180 (wood)chuck	245 lunch
stuck		feeding	246–251
		181	252 single
		182 ripe	253–254
		183	
		184 (any)body	